Anderson adores happy endings, so you can [...]
[...] you've got happy endings to enjoy when you [...]
[...]r books, she promises nothing less. She loves [...]
[...]rmint-filled dark chocolate, pineapple juice & [...]
[...]mely long showers, plus teasing her imaginary [...]
[...]ds with dating dilemmas! She lives in New Zealand [...]
[...] her gorgeous husband & four fabulous children. [...]
[...]u love happy endings too, come find her on [...]
[...]book.com/authornataliea, twitter @authornataliea, [...]
[...]atalie-anderson.com

PRINCESS'S PREGNANCY SECRET

NATALIE ANDERSON

MILLS & BOON

First Published in Great Britain 2018
by Mills & Boon, an imprint of HarperCollins*Publishers*
1 London Bridge Street, London, SE1 9GF

© 2018 Natalie Anderson

ISBN: 978-0-263-93441-0

To my family, for your patience, belief,
bad-but-good puns and supreme fun…

We are such an awesome team,
and I am so very lucky.

CHAPTER ONE

DAMON GALE STALKED the perimeter of the crowded ballroom, dodging another cluster of smiling women whose feathered masks neither softened nor hid their hunger as they stared at him.

He shouldn't have discarded his mask so soon.

Turning his back on another wordless invitation, he sipped his champagne, wishing it contained a stronger liquor. Women wanted more from him than he ever wanted from them. Always. While they agreed to a fling—fully informed of his limits—when it ended, recriminations and resentment came.

You're heartless.

He smiled cynically as the echo rang in his head. His last ex had thrown that old chestnut at him in a few months ago. And, yes, he was. Heartless and happy with it.

And what did it matter? For tonight business, not pleasure, beckoned. Tonight he was drawing a line beneath a decades-old disaster and tomorrow he'd walk away from this gilded paradise without a backwards glance. Just coming back had made old wounds hurt like fresh hits.

But for now he'd endured the outrageously opulent entrance, navigated his way up the marble staircase and walked through not one but five antechambers. Each room was larger and more ornate than the last, until finally he'd reached this gleaming monstrosity of a ballroom. The internal balcony overlooking the vast room already brimmed with celebrities and socialites eager to display themselves and spy on others.

Palisades palace was designed to reflect the glory of the royal family and make the average commoner feel as inconsequential as possible. It was supposed to invoke awe and envy. Frankly all the paintings, tapestries and gilded carvings exhausted Damon's eyes. He itched to ditch his dinner jacket and hit one of the trail runs along the pristine coastline that he far preferred to this sumptuous palace, but he needed to stay and play nice for just a little while longer.

Gritting his teeth, he turned away from the lens of an official photographer. He had no desire to feature in any-one's social media feed or society blog. He'd been forced to attend too many of these sorts of occasions in years past, as the proof of the supposed strength of his parents' union and thus to maximise any political inroads they could make from their connections.

The bitterness of their falsity soured the champagne.

Fortunately *his* career wasn't dependent upon the inter-est and approval of the wealthy and powerful. Thanks to his augmented reality software company, he was as wealthy as any of the patrons in attendance at this palace tonight. But even so, he was here to make the old-school grace and fa-vour system work for him just this once. Grimly he glanced over to where he'd left his half-sister only ten minutes ago. The investors he'd introduced her to were actively listening to her earnest, intelligent conversation, asking questions, clearly interested in what she was saying.

That introduction was all she'd agreed to accept from him. She'd refused his offer to fund her research himself and, while it irritated him, he didn't blame her. After all, they barely knew each other and neither of them wanted to dwell on the cancerous and numerous scars of their par-ents' infidelities. She had her pride and he respected her for it. But he'd been determined to try to help heal two de-cades of hurt and heartache caused by lies and deception, even in some small way, given his father's total lack of re-morse. From the intensity of that discussion, it seemed his job was done.

Now Damon turned away from the crowds, seeking solace in solitude for a moment before he could escape completely.

Symmetrical marble columns lined the length of the room. On one side they bracketed doors to the internal courtyard currently lit by lights strung in the trees. But on the other side the columns stood like sentries guarding shadowy alcoves.

A wisp of blue caught his eye as he approached the nearest column and he veered nearer. A woman stood veiled in the recess, her attention tightly focused on a group of revellers a few feet away. Her hair was ten shades of blue, hung to her waist and was most definitely a wig. A feathery mask covered half her face like an intimate web of black lace. Her shoulders, cheekbones and lips sparkled in a swirling combination of blue and silver powder.

Damon paused, unable to ignore the way her long dress emphasised every millimetre of her lithe body, clinging to her luscious curves and long legs. Despite that sparkling powder, he could see the tan of her skin and it suggested she was more mermaid than wait. She definitely spent time in the sun and that toned body didn't come from sitting on a spread towel doing nothing.

She was fit—in all interpretations of the word—but it was her undeniable femininity that stole his breath. Her pointed chin and high cheekbones and perfectly pouted lips were pure prettiness and delicacy, while her bountiful breasts were barely contained in the too-tight bodice of her midnight-blue dress.

She hadn't noticed him as she stood still and alone, watching the crowd. So he watched her. Her mask didn't hide her emotions—while her intentions were not obvious, her anxiety was. Something about her stark isolation softened that hard knot tied fast in his chest and set a challenge at the same time.

He was seized by the desire to make her smile.

He was also seized by the urge to span his hands around her narrow waist and pull her close so he could feel the graceful combination of softness and strength that her figure promised.

He smiled ruefully as raw warmth coursed through his veins. Its unexpected ferocity was vastly better than the cold ash clogging his lungs when he'd first arrived. Perhaps there could be a moment of pleasure here after all, now his business was concluded and that personal debt paid.

He quietly strolled nearer. Her attention was still fixed on the people gathering in the glittering ballroom, but he focused on her. She hovered on the edge of the room, still in the shadow. Still almost invisible to everyone else.

Her breasts swelled as she inhaled deeply. He hesitated, waiting for her to move forward. But contrary to his expectation, she suddenly stepped back, her expression falling as she turned away.

Damon narrowed his gaze. He had his own reasons for avoiding occasions like this, but why would a beautiful young woman like her want to hide? She should have company.

He lifted a second glass from the tray of a passing waiter and stepped past the column into the alcove. She'd paused in her retreat to look over that vast room of bejewelled, beautiful people. The expression in her eyes was obvious, despite the mask and the make-up. Part longing, part loneliness, her isolation stirred him. He spoke before thinking better of it.

'Can't quite do it?'

She whirled to face him, her eyes widening. Damon paused, needing a moment to appreciate the layers of sequins and powder on her pretty features. She was so very blue. She registered the two glasses he was holding and darted a glance behind him. As she realised he was alone, her eyes widened more. He smiled at her obvious wariness.

'It's your first time?' he asked.

Her mouth opened in a small wordless gasp.

'At the palace,' he clarified, wryly amused while keenly aware of the fullness of her glittered lips. 'It can be overwhelming the first time.'

Fascinatingly a telltale colour ran up her neck and face, visible despite the artful swirls of powder dusting almost every inch of her exposed skin. She was *blushing* at the most innocuous of statements.

Well, almost innocuous.

His smile deepened as he imagined her response if he were to utter something a great deal more inappropriate. Her body captured his attention, and he couldn't resist stealing a glance lower.

Heat speared again, tightening his muscles. He dragged his gaze up and realised she'd caught his slip. Unabashed he smiled again, letting her know in that time-worn way of his interest. She met his open gaze, not stepping back. But still she said nothing.

Alone. Definitely unattached. And almost certainly on the inexperienced side.

Damon hadn't chased a woman in a long while. Offers from more than willing bedmates meant he was more hunted than hunter. He avoided their attempts to snare him for longer, bored with justifying his refusal to commit to a relationship. He had too much of what women wanted— money and power. And yes, physical stamina and experience. Women enjoyed those things too.

But the possibilities here were tempting—when she reacted so tantalisingly with so little provocation? Those too-blue eyes and that too-sombre pout were beguiling.

He'd barely expected to stay ten minutes, let alone find someone who'd rouse his playful side. But now his obligation to Kassie had been met, he had the urge to amuse himself.

'What's your name?' he asked.

Her pupils dilated as if she was surprised but, again, she said nothing.

'I think I'll call you "Blue",' he said leisurely.

Her chin lifted fractionally. 'Because of my hair?'

He had to stop his jaw from dropping at the sound of her husky tones. That sultriness was at complete odds with her innocent demeanour. She was as raspy as a kitten's tongue. The prospect of making her purr tightened his interest.

'Because of the longing in your eyes.' And because of the pout of her pretty mouth.

'What do you think I'm longing for?'

Now there was a question. One he chose not to answer, knowing his silence would speak for itself. He just looked at her—feeling the awareness between them snap.

'What should I call you?' she asked after a beat.

He lifted his eyebrows. 'You don't know who I am?'

Her lips parted as she shook her head. 'Should I?'

He studied her for a moment—there had been no flash of recognition in her eyes when he'd first spoken to her, and there was none now. How...*refreshing*. 'No,' he said. 'I'm no one of importance. No prince, that's for sure.'

Something flickered in her eyes then, but it was gone before he could pick it up.

'I'm visiting Palisades for a few days,' he drawled. 'And I'm single.'

Her lips parted. 'Why do I need to know that?'

That sultry voice pulled, setting off a small ache deep in his bones. He didn't much like aches. He preferred action.

'No reason.' He shrugged carelessly, but smiled.

Her lips twitched, then almost curved. Satisfaction seeped into his gut, followed hard by something far hotter. Pleasure. It pressed him closer.

'Why are you all alone in here?' He offered her the second glass of champagne.

She accepted it but took such a small sip he wasn't

sure that the liquid even hit her lips. A careful woman. Intriguing.

'Are you hiding?' he queried.

She licked her lips and glanced down at her dress before tugging at the strap that was straining to hold her curves.

Definitely nervous.

'You look beautiful,' he added. 'You don't need to worry about that.'

That wave of colour swept her cheeks again but she lifted her head. There was an assuredness in her gaze now that surprised him. 'I'm not worried about that.'

Oh? So she held a touch more confidence than had first appeared. Another shot of satisfaction rushed. His fingers itched with the urge to tug the wig from her head and find out what colour her hair really was. While this façade was beautiful, it was a fantasy he wanted to pierce so he could see the real treasure beneath.

'Then why aren't you out there?' he asked.

'Why aren't you?' Alert, she watched for his response.

'Sometimes attendance at these things is *necessary* rather than desired.'

'These "things"?' she mocked his tone.

'It depends who's here.'

'No doubt you desire these "things" more when there are plenty of pretty women.' She was breathless beneath that rasp.

But he knew she was enjoying this slight spar and parry. He'd play along.

'Naturally.' Damon coolly watched her over the rim of his glass as he sipped his drink, deliberately hiding his delight. 'I am merely a man, after all.' He shrugged helplessly.

Her gaze narrowed on him, twin sparks shooting from that impossible blue. 'You mean you're a boy who likes playing with toys. A doll here, a doll there…'

'Of course,' he followed her smoothly. 'Toying with dolls can be quite an amusing pastime. As can collecting them.'

'I'll bet.'

He leaned forward, deliberately intruding into intimate space to whisper conspiratorially, 'I never break my toys though,' he promised. 'I take very good care when I'm playing.'

'Oh?' Her gaze lanced straight through his veneer, striking at a weak spot he didn't know he had. 'If you say it, it must be true.'

Appreciating her little flash of spirit, he was instantly determined to take very great care…to torture her delightfully.

'And you?' he asked, though he already suspected the answer. 'Do you often attend nights like this?' Did she play with toys of her own?

She shrugged her shoulders in an echo of his.

He leaned closer again, rewarded as he heard the hitch in her breathing. 'Do you work at the hospital?'

Tonight's ball was the annual fundraiser and, while he knew huge amounts were raised, it was also the chance for hospital staff to be celebrated.

'I…do some stuff there.' Her lashes lowered.

Wasn't she just Ms Mysterious? 'So why aren't you with your friends?'

'I don't know them all that well.'

Perhaps she was a new recruit who'd won an invitation for this ball in the ballot they held for the hospital staff. Perhaps that was why she didn't have any friends with her. It wouldn't take long for her to find a few. Some surgeon would snap her up if he had any sense. Then it wouldn't be long before she lost that arousing ability to blush.

A spear of possessiveness shafted through him at the thought of some other guy pulling her close. Surprising him into taking another step nearer to her. Too near.

'Do you want to dance?' He gave up on subtlety altogether.

She glanced beyond him. 'No one is dancing yet.'

'We could start the trend.'

She quickly shook her head, leaning back into the shadows so his body hid her from those in the ballroom. Damon guessed she didn't want to stand out. Too late, to him she already did.

'Don't be intimidated by any of that lot.' He jerked his head towards the crowds. 'They might have the wealth but they don't always have the manners. Or the kindness.'

'You're saying you don't fit in either?' The scepticism in her gaze as she looked him over was unmissable.

He resisted the urge to preen in front of her like some damn peacock. Instead he offered a platitude. 'Does anyone truly fit in?'

Her gaze flashed up to his and held it a long moment. Her irises were such a vibrant blue he knew they had to be covered with contacts. The pretence of polite small talk fell away. The desire to reach for her—to strip her—almost overwhelmed him. Now *that* was inappropriate. He tensed, pushing back the base instinct. Damn, he wanted to touch her. Wanted her to touch him. That look in her eyes? Pure invitation. Except he had the feeling she was too inexperienced to even be aware of it.

But he couldn't stop the question spilling roughly from his lips. 'Are you going to do it?'

Eleni Nicolaides didn't know what or how to answer him. This man wasn't like anyone she'd met before.

Direct. Devastating. *Dangerous.*

'Are you going to do it, Blue?'

'Do what?' she whispered vaguely, distracted by the play of dark and light in his watchful expression. He was appallingly handsome in that tall, dark, sex-on-a-stick sort of way. The kind of obviously experienced playboy who'd never been allowed near her.

But at the same time there was more than that to him—something that struck a chord within her. A new—seductive—note that wasn't purely because of the physical magnetism of the man.

He captivated every one of her senses and all her interest. A lick of something new burned—yearning. She wanted him closer. She wanted to reach out and touch him. Her pulse throbbed, beating need about her body—to her dry, sensitive lips, to her tight, full breasts, to other parts too secret to speak of...

His jaw tightened. Eleni blinked at the fierce intensity that flashed in his eyes. Had he read her mind? Did he know just *what* she wanted to do right now?

'Join in,' he answered between gritted teeth.

She swallowed. Now her pulse thundered as she realised how close she'd come to making an almighty fool of herself. 'I shouldn't...'

'Why not?'

So many reasons flooded her head in a cacophony of panic.

Her disguise, her deceit, her *duty*.

'Blue?' he prompted. His smile was gentle enough but the expression in his eyes was too hot.

Men had looked at her with lust before, but those times the lust hadn't been for her but for her wealth, her title, her virtue. She'd never been on a date. She was totally untouched. And everyone knew. She'd read the crude conjecture and the jokes in the lowest of the online guttersnipes: *THE VIRGIN PRINCESS!!!*

All caps. Multiple exclamation marks.

That her 'purity' was so interesting and so important angered her. It wasn't as if it had been deliberate. It wasn't as if she'd saved herself for whichever prince would be chosen for her to marry. She'd simply been so sequestered there'd been zero chance to find even a friend, let alone a boyfriend.

And now it transpired that her Prince was to be Xander of the small European state of Santa Chiara. He certainly hadn't saved himself for her and she knew his fidelity after their marriage was not to be expected. Discretion was, but not that sort of intimate loyalty. Or love.

'Do you ever stop asking questions?' she asked, trying for cool and sophisticated for these last few moments of escape.

Wishing she could be as accepting as so many others who didn't doubt their arranged marriages. Because this was it. Tomorrow her engagement would be formally announced. A man she'd barely met and most certainly didn't like would become her fiancé. She felt frigid at the thought. But those archaic royal rules remained unchallenged and offered certainty. The Princess of Palisades could never marry a commoner. This disguise tonight was a lame leap for five minutes of total freedom. The only five minutes she'd have.

'Not if I'm curious about something.'

'And you're curious about—'

'You. Unbearably. Yes.'

Heat slammed into every cell. She couldn't hold his gaze but she couldn't look away either. His eyes were truly blue—not enhanced by contacts the way hers were—and hot. He seemed to see right through her mask, her carefully applied powder, her whole disguise. He saw the need she'd tried to hide from everyone.

She was out of place and yet this was her home—where she'd been born and raised and where her future was destined, dictated by duty.

'You have the chance to experience this…' he waved at the ballroom full of beautiful people '…yet you're hanging back in the shadows.'

He voiced her fantasy—reminding her of her stupid,

crazy plan. She'd arranged for a large selection of costumes to be delivered to the nurses' quarters at the hospital for tonight's masquerade. No one would know that one dress, one wig, and one mask were missing from that order. All done so she, cloistered, protected, precious Princess Eleni, could steal one night as an anonymous girl able to talk to people not as a princess, but as a nobody.

She could be no one.

And yet, when it had come to it, she'd swiftly realised her error. She'd watched those guests arrive. Clustered together, laughing squads of *friends*—the kind she'd never had. How could she walk into that room and start talking to any of them *without* her title as her armour? What had she to offer? How could she blend in when she hadn't any clue what to discuss other than superficial niceties? She'd ached with isolation, inwardly mocking her own self-piteous hurt, as she'd uselessly stared at all those other carefree, relaxed people having fun.

Privileged Princess Eleni had burned with jealousy.

Now she burned with something else, something just as shameful.

'I'm biding my time,' she prevaricated with a chuckle, drawing on years of practising polite conversation to cover her shaken, unruly emotions.

'You're wasting it.'

His bluntness shocked that smile from her lips. She met his narrowed gaze and knew he saw too much.

'You want a night out, you need to get out there and start circulating,' he advised.

Her customary serene demeanour snapped at his tone. 'Maybe that's not what I want.'

The atmosphere pulsed between them like an electrical charge faulting.

Heat suffused every inch of her skin. Now she truly was unable to hold his gaze. But as she looked down he reached out. The merest touch of fingers to her chin, nudging so she looked him in the eye again. She fought to quell the uncontrollable shiver that the simple touch generated.

'No?' Somehow he was even closer as he quietly pressed her. 'Then what do you want?'

That she couldn't answer. Not to herself. Not now. But he could see it anyway.

'Walk with me through the ballroom,' he said in a low voice. 'I dare you.'

His challenge roused a rare surge of rebellion within her. She who always did as she was bid—loyal, dutiful, serene. Princess Eleni never caused trouble. But *he* stirred trouble. Her spirit lifted; she was determined to show strength before him.

'I don't need you to dare me,' she breathed.

'Don't you?' He called her bluff.

Silent, she registered the gauntlet in his hard gaze. The glow of those blue eyes ignited her to mutinous action. She turned and strode to the edge of the alcove. Nerves thrummed, chilling her. What if she was recognised?

But this man hadn't recognised her and she knew her brother would be busy in the farthest corner of the room meeting select guests at this early stage in the evening. Everyone was preoccupied with their own friends and acquaintances. She *might* just get away with this after all.

'Coming?' She looked back and asked him, refusing—yet failing—to flush.

He took her hand and placed it in the crook of his elbow, saying nothing, but everything, with a sardonic look. The rock-hard heat of his biceps seeped through the fine material of his tailored suit and her fingers curled around it instinctively. He pressed his arm close to his side, trapping her hand.

He walked slowly, deliberately, the length of the colonnades. To her intense relief, he didn't stop to speak to anyone, instead he kept his attention on her, his gaze melting that cold block of nervousness lodged in her diaphragm.

It turned out she'd been wrong to worry about recognition. Because while people *were* looking, it was not at her.

'All these women are watching you,' she murmured as they drew near the final column. 'And they look surprised.'

A smile curled his sensual lips. 'I haven't been seen dating recently.'

'They think I'm your date?' she asked. 'Am I supposed to feel flattered?'

His laughter was low and appreciative. 'Don't deny it, you do.'

She pressed her lips together, refusing to smile. But the sound of his laugh wasn't just infectious, it seemed to reach right inside her and chase all that cold away with its warmth.

'There.' He drew her into the last alcove, a mirror of the first, and she was appallingly relieved to discover it too was empty at this early hour.

'Was that so awful?' he asked, not relinquishing her hand but walking with her to the very depths of the respite room and turning to face her.

Inwardly she was claiming it as a bittersweet victory. A date at last.

'Who are you?' She felt foolish that she didn't know when it was clear many others did. 'Why do they look at you?'

He cocked his head, his amusement gleaming. 'Why do *you* look at me?'

Eleni refused to answer. She was *not* going to pander to his already outsize ego.

His lazy smile widened. 'What do you see?'

That one she could answer. She smiled, relishing her release from 'polite princess response'.

'I see arrogance,' she answered boldly. 'A man who defies convention and doesn't give a damn what anyone thinks.'

'Because?'

She angled her head, mirroring his inquiring look. 'You don't wear a mask. You don't make the effort that's expected of everyone else.'

'And I don't do that—because why?' His attention narrowed—laser-like in its focus on her.

'Because you don't need to,' she guessed, seeing the appreciation flicker in his eyes. 'You don't want their approval. You're determined to show you don't need *anything* from them.'

His expression shuttered, but he didn't deny her assessment of him. Her heart quickened as he stepped closer.

'Do you know what I see?' Almost angrily he pointed to the mask covering most of her face. 'I see someone hiding more than just her features. I see a woman who wants more than what she thinks she should have.'

She stilled, bereft—of speech, of spirit. Because she did want more and yet she knew she was so spoilt and selfish to do so. She had *everything*, didn't she?

'So what happens at midnight?' That tantalising smile quirked his lips, drawing her attention to the sensuality that was such a potent force within him.

She struggled to remind herself she was no Cinderella. She was already the Princess, after all. 'Exactly what you think it will.'

'You'll leave and I'll never see you again.'

His words struck deep inside her—sinking like stones of regret.

'Precisely,' she replied with her perfectly practised princess politeness.

She shouldn't feel the slightest disappointment. This was merely a fleeting conversation in the shadows. Five minutes of dalliance that she could reminisce over a whole lot later. Like for the rest of her life.

'I don't believe in fairy tales,' he said roughly, his smile lost.

'Nor do I,' she whispered. She believed in duty. In family. In doing what was right. Which was why she was going to marry a man she didn't love and who didn't love her. Romance was for fairy tales and other people.

'You sure about that?' He edged closer still, solemn and intense. 'Then flip it. Don't do the expected. Don't disappear at midnight.' He dared her with that compelling whisper. 'Stay and do what you want. You have the mask to protect you. *Take* what you want.'

She stared up at him. He was roguishly handsome and he was only playing with her, wasn't he? But that was…okay. Intense temptation and a totally foreign sensation rippled through her. The trickle soon turned into a tsunami. From the deepest core of her soul, slipping along her veins to ignite every inch of her body.

Want.

Pure and undeniable.

Couldn't she have just a very little moment for herself? Couldn't she have just a very little of *him*?

He couldn't hide his deepening tension. It was in his eyes, in the single twitch of the muscle in his jaw as the curve of his smile flatlined. That infinitesimal *edge* sharpened. But he remained as motionless as the marble column behind him, hiding the ballroom from her view. Waiting, watching.

Take what you want.

That dare echoed in her mind, fuelling her desire.

She gazed into his eyes, losing herself in the molten steel. She parted her lips the merest fraction to draw in a desperate breath. But he moved the moment she did. Full predator—fast, powerful, inescapable—he pressed his mouth to meet hers.

Instinctively she closed her eyes, unable to focus on anything but the sensation of his warm lips teasing hers. Her breath caught as he stepped closer, his hands spanning her waist to draw her against him. She quivered on impact as she felt his hard strength, finally appreciating the sheer size of the man. Tall, strong, he radiated pure masculinity.

He took complete control, his tongue sliding along her lips, slipping past to stroke her. Never had she been kissed like this. Never had *she* kissed like this, but his commanding passion eviscerated any insecurity—and all thought. Lost to the sensation she simply leaned closer, letting him support her, pressing her into his iron heat.

Heavy, addictive power flowed from him to her as he kissed the very soul of her. His arms were like bars, drawing her against the solid expanse of his chest. A moan rose in the back of her throat and he tightened his hold more. She quivered at his defined strength—not just physical. It took mental strength to build a body like his, she knew that too.

Her legs weakened even as a curious energy surged through her. She needed him closer still. But his hand lifted to cup her jaw and he teased—pressing maddeningly light kisses on her lips instead of that explosive, carnal kiss of before. She moaned, in delight, in frustration.

At that raw, unbidden response, he gave her what she wanted. Uncontrolled passion. She clutched at him wildly as her knees gave out—swept away on a torrent of need that had somehow been unleashed. She didn't know how to assuage it, how to combat it. All she could do was cling— wordlessly, mindlessly begging for more. The intensity of his desire mirrored her own—she felt him brace, felt the burning of his skin beneath her fingertips as she touched his jaw, copying his delightful touch.

But now his hand stroked lower, pressing against her thigh. Breathless she slipped deeper, blindly seeking more. But she felt his hesitation. She gasped as he broke the kiss to look at her. Unthinking she arched closer, seeking to regain contact. But in the distance she heard a roaring. A clinking of—

Glasses. *Guests*.

Good grief, what was she *doing*?

Far too late those years of training, duty and responsibility kicked in. How could she have forgotten who and where she was? She could not throw everything away for one moment of *lust*.

But this lust was all-consuming. All she wanted was for him to touch her again—decisively, intimately, now.

Brutal shame burned from her bones to her skin. She had to get alone and under control. But as she twisted from his hold a long tearing sound shredded the unnatural silence between them. Time slowed as realisation seeped into her fried brain.

That too tight, too thin strap over her shoulder had ripped clear from the fabric it had been straining to support. And the result?

She didn't need to look to know; she could feel the exposure—the cooler air on her skin. Aghast, she sent him a panicked glance. Had he noticed?

Of course he'd noticed.

She froze, transfixed, as his gaze rested for a second longer on her bared breast before flicking back to her face. The fiery hunger in his eyes consumed her. She was alight with colour and heat, but it wasn't embarrassment.

Oh, heavens, no.

She tugged up the front of her dress and turned, blindly seeking escape.

But he drew her close again, bracketing her into the protective stance of his body. He walked, pressing her forward away from the crowd she'd foolishly forgotten was present. And she was so confused she just let him. Through a discreet archway, down a wide corridor to space and silence. He walked with her, until a door closed behind them.

The turn of the lock echoed loudly. Startled, she turned to see him jerkily stripping out of his dinner jacket with barely leashed violence. His white dress shirt strained across his broad shoulders. Somehow he seemed bigger, more aggressive, more sexual.

Appallingly desire flooded again, rooting her to the spot where she clutched her torn dress to her chest. She desperately tried to catch her breath but her body couldn't cope. Her lips felt full and sensitive and throbbed for the press of his. Her breasts felt tight and heavy and, buried deep within, she was molten hot and aching.

All she could do was stare as he stalked towards her.

All she could think was to surrender.

CHAPTER TWO

'SLIP THIS AROUND your shoulders and we can leave immediately.' He held the jacket out to her. 'No one will...' He trailed off as she stared at him uncomprehendingly.

He'd only been stripping in order to *clothe* her? To protect her from prying eyes rather than continue with...with...

Suddenly she was mortified. She'd thought that he'd been going to—

'*No.*' She finally got her voice box to work. 'No. That's impossible.'

Nervously she licked her lips. What was impossible was her own reaction. Her own *willingness*. Horrified, she stepped away from the temptation personified in front of her, backing up until she was almost against the wall on the far side of the room.

He stood still, his jacket gently swinging from his outstretched hand, and watched her move away from him. A slight frown furrowed his forehead. Then he shifted, easing his stance. He casually tossed the jacket onto the antique sofa that now stood between them.

His lips twisted with a smile as rueful as it was seductive. 'I'm not going to do anything.'

'I know,' she said quickly, trying and failing to offer a smile in return.

She wasn't afraid of him. She was afraid of herself. Her cheeks flamed and she knew a fierce blush had every inch of her skin aglow. Shamed, she clutched the material closer to her chest.

This had been such a mistake. More dangerous than she ever could have imagined. Her breathing quickened again. She was so mortified but so *sensitive*. She glanced at him again only to have him snare her gaze in his. He was watching her too intently. She realised that his breathing was quickened, like hers, and a faint sheen highlighted his sun-kissed skin.

'Are you okay?' he asked softly. 'I'm sorry.'

But he didn't look sorry. If anything that smile deepened.

But she also saw the intensity of the heat banked in his expression and something unfurled within her. Something that didn't help her resistance.

'It wasn't your fault,' she muttered. 'It's a cheap dress and it doesn't really fit that well.'

'Let me help you fix it,' he offered huskily. 'So you can get out of here.'

'I can make do.' She glanced at the locked door behind him. 'I'd better go.'

She knew there was another exit from the room, but it was locked by the security system. She couldn't use it without showing him she was intimate with the palace layout. He could never know that. Maybe she could drape the blue and purple hair of her wig over her shoulder to hide that tear.

'Trust me,' he invited gruffly. 'I'll fix your dress. Won't do anything else.'

That was the problem. She wanted him to do something. Do *everything* or *anything* he wanted. And that was just crazy because she couldn't set a lifetime of responsibility ablaze now. What made it worse was that he knew—why she'd moved to put not just space, but furniture between them.

'You can't get past them all with that strap the way it is now,' he muttered.

He was right. She couldn't get away from him either. Not yet.

So she stepped nearer, turning to present her shoulder with the torn strap. 'Thank you.'

Holding her breath, heart pounding, she fought to remain

still as he came within touching distance. The tips of his deft fingers brushed against her burning skin as he tried to tie the loose strap to the torn bodice. She felt it tighten, but then heard his sharp mutter of frustration as the strap loosened again.

She inhaled a jagged breath. 'Don't worry—'

'I'll get it this time,' he interrupted. 'Almost there.'

She waited, paralysed, as he bent to the task again, trying desperately to quell her responsive shiver to the heat of his breath on her skin but he noticed it anyway. His hands stilled for that minuscule moment before working again.

'There,' he promised in a lethal whisper. 'All fixed.'

But he was still there—too close, too tall, too everything. She stood with her eyes tight shut, totally aware of him.

'You're good to go.'

Good. She didn't feel like being good. And she didn't want to go.

She opened her eyes and saw what she'd already felt with every other sense. He was close enough to kiss.

She shook her head very slightly, not wanting to break this spell. 'It was a dumb idea. I shouldn't have come.'

She hadn't meant to tell him anything more but the secret simply fell from her lips.

'But you've gone to such trouble.' He traced one of the swirls of glitter she'd painted on her shoulder. His finger roved north, painting another that rose up her neck, near her frantically beating pulse, and rested there.

'You shouldn't miss out.' He didn't break eye contact as he neared, but he didn't close the half-inch between their mouths.

She had to miss out. That was her destiny—the rules set before she was even born. Yet his gaze mesmerised, making her want all kinds of impossible things. Beneath those thick lashes the intensity of his truly blue eyes burned through to her core.

'You'd better get back out there, Blue.' He suddenly broke the taut silence and dropped his hand. His voice roughened, almost as if he were angry.

'Why?' Why should she? When what she wanted was right here? Just one more kiss? Just once? Hot fury speared—the fierce emotion striking all sense from her. 'Maybe I can…' she muttered, gazing into his eyes.

'Can what?' he challenged, arching an eyebrow. 'What can you do…?'

She tilted her chin and reached up on tiptoe to brush her lips over his. Sensation shivered through her. This was right. This was *it*.

He stiffened, then took complete control. He gripped her waist and hauled her close, slamming her body into his. She felt the give of her stupid dress again. She didn't mind the half-laugh that heated her.

'You can do that,' he muttered, a heated tease as he kissed her with those torturous light kisses until she moaned in frustration. 'You can do that all you like.'

She did like. She liked it a *lot*.

Kisses. Nothing wrong with kisses. Her bodice fluttered down again, exposing her to him. Thank goodness. His hands took advantage, then his mouth. The drive for more overwhelmed her. Never had she felt so alive. Or so good.

She gasped when he lifted her, but she didn't resist, didn't complain. He strode a couple of paces to sit on the sofa, crushing her close then settling her astride his lap.

She shivered in delight as he kissed her again. She could die in these kisses. She met every one, mimicking, learning, becoming braver. Becoming unbearably aroused. Breathless, she lost all sense of time—could only succumb to the sensation as his hand swept down her body, down her legs. Slowly he drew up the hem of her dress. His fingertips stroked up her hot skin until he neared that most private part of her. She shivered and he lifted his head, looking deep into her eyes. She knew he was seeking permission.

She wriggled ever so slightly to let him have greater access because this felt too good to stop. Still watching her, he slid his hand higher.

'Kiss me again,' she whispered.

Something flared in his eyes. And kiss her he did, but not on her mouth. He bent lower, drawing her nipple into the hot cavern of his mouth while at the same time his fingertips erotically teased over the crotch of her panties.

Eleni gasped and writhed—seeking both respite from the torment, and more of it. No one had touched her so intimately. And, heaven have mercy, she liked it.

She caught a glimpse of the reflection in the mirror hanging on the opposite wall. She didn't recognise the woman with that man bending to her bared breasts. This was one stranger doing deliciously naughty things with another stranger—kissing and rubbing and touching and sliding. Beneath her, his hard length pressed against his suit pants. It fascinated her. The devilish ache to explore him more overtook her. She rocked against his hand, shivering with forbidden delight. She was so close to something, but she was cautious. He pulled back for a second and studied her expression. She clenched her jaw. She didn't want him to stop.

'Take what you want,' he urged softly. 'Whatever you want.'

'I...'

'Anything,' he muttered. 'As much or as little as you like.'

Because he wanted this too. She felt the tremble in his fingers and it gave her confidence. Somehow she knew he was as taken aback as she by this conflagration. She might not have the experience, but she had the intuition to understand this was physical passion at its strongest.

Her legs quivered but she let him slide the satin skirt of her dress higher. It glided all the way up to her waist, exposing her almost completely. Her legs were bared, her chest, only her middle was covered in a swathe of blue. She sighed helplessly as that hard ridge of him pressed where she was aching most.

She struggled to unfasten his shirt buttons; she wanted to see his skin. To feel it. He helped her, pulling the halves of his shirt apart. For a moment she just stared. She'd known he was strong, she'd felt that. But the definition of his tense muscles—the pecs, the abs—still took her by surprise. The light scattering of hair added to the perfection. He was the ultimate specimen of masculinity. She raised her gaze, meeting the fire in his, and understood the strength he was holding in check.

'Touch all you like,' he muttered, a guttural command.

She liked it *all*. Suddenly stupidly nervous, she pressed her palm over his chest—feeling the hardness and heat of him. But she could feel the thump of his heart too and somehow that grounded her. She read the desire in his eyes, intuitively understanding how leashed his passion was. That he, like she, wanted it *all*.

'Touch me,' she choked. Her command—and his reply—dislodged the last brick in the wall that had been damming her desire inside. She did not want him to hold back with her.

He caressed her breasts with his hands, teasing her as she rocked on him, rubbing in the way the basic instinct of her body dictated—back and forth and around.

'So good,' she muttered, savouring the pressure of his mouth, the sweep of his hands, the hardness of him under her. 'So good.'

It was so foreign. So delicious. Feverish with desire, she arched. Pleasure beyond imagination engulfed her as faster they moved together. Kisses became ravenous. Hands swept hard over skin. Heat consumed her. She moaned, her head falling back as he touched her in places she'd never been touched. As he brought her sensuality to life.

She heard a tearing sound and realised it had been the

crotch of her panties. They'd not survived the strength of his grip. She glanced and saw he'd tossed the remnants of white silk and lace onto the wide seat. Now she could feel his hand touching her again so much more intimately.

'Oh.'

She dragged in a searing breath and gazed into his eyes.

'That's it, Blue,' he enticed her in that devilish whisper. 'Come on.'

She couldn't answer—not as his fingers circled, and slipped along the slick cleft of her sex, not as they teased that sensitive nub over and over and over. She bit her lip as that searing tension deep in her belly tightened. She rocked, her rhythm matching the pace of his fingers as they strummed over and around her. He kissed her, his tongue soothing the indent of her teeth on her lip, then stroking inside her mouth in an intimate exploration of her private space. Just as his finger probed within her too.

She tore her mouth from his and threw her head back, arching in agony as she gasped for breath. He fixed his mouth on her breast, drawing her nipple in deep. Pleasure shot from one sensitive point to another, rolling in violent waves across her body. She shuddered in exquisite agony, crying out as she was completely lost to this raw, writhing bliss.

When she opened her eyes she saw he was watching her, his hand gently stroking her thigh.

She breathed out, summoning calm and failing. Giddy, she gazed at him, stunned by the realisation that she'd just had an orgasm. She'd let him touch her and kiss her and he'd made the most amazing feelings flood through her. But the hunger had returned already and brought that special kind of anger with it.

That emptiness blossomed, bigger than before. There was more to this electricity between them. More that she'd missed. More that she wanted.

A chasm stretched before her. A choice. A line that, once

crossed, could never be reclaimed. But it was *her* choice. And suddenly she knew exactly how she wanted this one thing in her life to be. Within her control.

For this first time—for only this time—she wanted physical intimacy with a man who truly wanted her back. A man who wanted not her title, not her purity or connections. Just her—naked and no one special. This man knew nothing of who or what she was, but he wanted her. This was not love, no. But pure, basic, brilliant lust.

Just this once, she would be *wanted* for nothing but herself.

Almost angrily she shifted on him, pressing close again, kissing him. He kissed her back, as hard, as passionate. She moaned in his mouth. *Willing* him to take over. But he drew back, pressing his hand over hers, stopping her from sliding her palm down his chiselled chest to his belt.

'We're going to be in trouble in a second,' he groaned. 'Stop.'

She stared dazedly into his face as he eased her back along his thighs, almost crying at his rejection.

'I need to keep you safe,' he muttered as his hands worked quickly to release his zipper. 'One second. To be safe.'

She couldn't compute his comment because at that moment his erection sprang free. Never had she seen a man naked. Never had she *touched*. He reached into his trouser pocket and pulled out a small packet that he tore open with his teeth. Her mouth dried as she stared avidly.

Of course he was prepared. He was an incredibly handsome, virile man who knew exactly how to turn her on because *he* was experienced. He was used to this kind of anonymous tryst and he definitely knew how to make a woman feel good. And that was…*okay*.

As she tore her gaze away from the magnificence of him she caught sight of their reflections in that gleaming mirror again. The image of those two strangers—half naked and entwined—was the most erotic thing she'd ever seen in her life. Their pasts didn't matter. Nor did their futures. There was only this. Only them. Only now. She turned back to look at the overwhelming man she was sitting astride with such vulnerability—and with such desire.

Princess Eleni always did the right thing.

But she wasn't Princess Eleni tonight. She was no one and this was nothing.

'Easy, Blue.' He gently stroked her arm.

She realised her breathing was completely audible—rushed and short.

'Just whatever you want,' he muttered softly.

He wasn't just inviting her. He was giving her the choice, *all* the control. Yet his voice and his body both commanded and compelled her own and there was no choice.

This once. This *one* time. She wanted everything—all of him. She shimmied closer. The sight of his huge straining erection made her quiver and melt. She didn't know how to do this. She looked into his eyes and was lost in that intensity. And suddenly she understood.

She kissed him. Kissed him long and deep and softened in the delight. In the *rightness* of the sensation. She could feel him there beneath her. She rocked her hips, as she'd done before, feeling him slide through her feminine folds. His hands gripped her hips, holding her, helping her. She pressed down, right on that angle, every sense on high alert and anticipation. But her body resisted, unyielding.

She *wanted* this.

So she pushed down hard. Unexpectedly sharp pain pierced the heated fog of desire.

'Blue?' A burning statue beneath her; his breathing was ragged as he swore. 'I've—'

'I'm fine,' she pleaded, willing her body to welcome his.

'You're tight,' he said between gritted teeth.

'You're big.'

He filled her completely—beneath her, about her, within

her. The force and fire of his personality scalded her. Her
breath shuddered as she was locked in his embrace, and in
the intense heat of his gaze.

'Have I hurt you?' His question came clipped.

'No.' It wasn't regret that burned within her, but recognition. This was what she wanted. 'Kiss me.'

And he did. He kissed her into that pure state of bliss
once more. Into heat and light and sparkling rainbows and
all kinds of magic that were miraculous and new. Touching him ignited her and she moved restlessly, eager to feel
him touching her again too. That fullness between her legs
eased. Honeyed heat bloomed and she slid closer still to
him. She sighed, unable to remain still any more. His arms
tightened around her, clasping her to him as he kissed her
back—exactly how she needed. *Yes.* This was so good, it
had to be right. He shifted her, sliding her back, and then
down hard on the thick column of his manhood.

He suddenly stood, taking her weight with no apparent difficulty. Startled, she instinctively wrapped her legs
around his waist. He kissed her in approval and took those
few paces to where that narrow table stretched along the
wall. He stood at the short end and carefully placed her
right on the edge of it, then slowly he eased her so she lay
on her back on the cool wood. Her legs were wound around
his waist, her hips tilted upwards as he braced over her, his
shaft still driven to the hilt inside her. That mirror was right
beside her now but she didn't turn her head to look again
at those strangers; she couldn't. Her wicked rake claimed
every ounce of her focus.

'This is madness,' he muttered. 'But I don't care.'

Nor did she. This moment was too perfect. Too precious.
Too much to be denied.

His large hands cupped her, holding her as he pressed
into her deeply, and then pulled back a fraction, only to push
forward again. Again, then again, then again. Every time
he seemed to drive deeper, claiming more and more of her.

And she gave it to him. She would give him everything, he made her feel so good. He gazed into her eyes and in his she saw the echo of her own emotions—wonder, pleasure, *need*.

She'd never been as close to another person in all her life. Not so passionately, nakedly close. Nor so vulnerable, or so safe. Never so free.

She kissed him in arousal, in madness, in gratitude. Trusting him implicitly. He'd already proven his desire to please her.

'Come again,' he coaxed in a passionate whisper. 'I want to feel you come.'

She wanted that too. She wanted exactly that.

He touched her just above the point where they were joined, teasing even as he filled her. She gasped as she felt the sensations inside gather once more in that unstoppable storm.

'You…please…' she begged incoherently as she feverishly clutched him, digging her fingernails into his flesh. She wanted him to feel the same ecstasy surging through her. She needed him on this ride *with* her. As she frantically arched to meet him she heard his groan. His hands gripped tighter, his expression tensed. She smiled in that final second. She wanted to laugh. She wanted to revel in it and she never, ever wanted it to end.

His face flushed as sensation swept the final vestige of control from his grasp. Pleasure stormed through her again, surging to the farthest reaches of her body. She sobbed in the onslaught of goodness and delight and his roar of satisfaction was the coda to her completeness.

Her eyes were closed. She could hear only the beating of her heart and his as they recovered. She was pinned by his weight and it was the best feeling on earth.

But then laughter rang out. Not hers. Nor his.

'What's in this room?'

Eleni snapped her head to stare at the door as someone on the other side tried the handle.

'Hello?'

More laughter reverberated through the wood.

Reality returned in a violent slam, evaporating the mist of delight. Suddenly she saw herself as she'd look to anyone who burst through that door—Princess Eleni of Palisades, ninety per cent naked, sprawled on a table with her legs around the waist of some stranger and his body ploughed deep into hers.

Sordid headlines smashed into her head: *shameless wanton...a one-night stand...the eve of her engagement...* There would be no mercy, no privacy—only scorn and shame. She had to get out of here. Aghast, she stared up at the handsome stranger she'd just ravished. What had she done?

Damon watched his masked lover's eyes widen in shock. Beneath the blue sparkled powder, her skin paled and her kiss-crushed lips parted in a silent gasp. This was more than embarrassment. This was fear. He was so stunned by her devastated expression he stepped back. She slipped down from the table and tugged at her crumpled clothing. Before he could speak someone knocked on the door again. More voices sounded out in the corridor.

Her pallor worsened.

'I'll get rid of them,' he assured her, hauling up his trousers so he could get to the door and deny anyone entrance to the room. He was determined to wipe that terror from her face.

He pressed a hand on the door. Even though he'd locked it, he couldn't be sure someone wouldn't be able to unlock it from the other side. He listened intently, hoping the revellers would pass and go exploring elsewhere. After a few moments the voices faded.

He turned back to see how she was doing, but she'd vanished. Shocked, he stared around the empty room, then stalked back to where she'd been standing seconds ago.

Only now did he register the other door tucked to the side of that large mirror. There were two entrances to this room and he'd been so caught up in her he'd not even noticed.

He tried the handle but it was locked. So how had she got through it? Keenly he searched and spotted a discreet security screen. Had she known the code to get out? She must have. Because in the space of two seconds, she'd fled.

Just who was she? Why so afraid of someone finding her? Foreboding filled him. He didn't trust women. He didn't trust anyone.

If only he'd peeled off that mask and seen her face properly. How could he have made such a reckless, risky decision?

Anger simmered, but voices sounded outside the other door again, forcing him to move. He glanced in the mirror at his passion-swept reflection. Frowning, he swiftly buttoned his shirt and fixed his trousers properly. Thank heavens he'd retained enough sense to use protection. But as he sorted himself out he realised something he'd missed in his haste to ensure that door was secure. The damn condom was torn. And more than that? It was marked with a trace of something that shouldn't have been there. He remembered when she'd first pushed down on him. When she'd inhaled sharply and tears had sprung to her eyes.

Uncertainty. *Pain.*

Grimly he fastened his belt. He'd been too lost to lust to absorb the implications of her reaction. Now his gut tensed as he struggled to believe the evidence. Had she given him her virginity? Had she truly never had another lover and yet let him, a total stranger, have her in a ten-minute tryst in a private powder room?

Impossible. But the stain of her purity was on his skin. His pulse thundered in his ears. *Why* would she have done something so wild? What was her motivation?

Hell, what had *he* been thinking? To have had sex with

a woman he'd barely met as fast and as furiously as possible? Almost in public?

But her expressive response had swept all sensible thought from his head. She'd *wanted* him and heaven knew he'd wanted her. He was appalled by his recklessness; his anger roared. But a twist of Machiavellian satisfaction brewed beneath, because he was going to have to find her. He was going to have to warn her about the condom. The instinct to hunt her pressed like the blade of a knife. She owed him answers.

Find her. Find her. Find her.

His pulse banged like a pagan's drum, marching him back to the busy ballroom. He even took to the balcony to scan the braying crowd, determined to find that blue hair and swan-like neck. But he knew it was futile. The midnight hour had struck and that sizzling Cinderella had run away, never wanting to be seen again.

Least of all by him.

CHAPTER THREE

'YOU LOOK PEAKY.'

Eleni forced a reassuring smile and faced her brother across the aisle in his jet.

'I have a bit of a headache but it's getting better,' she lied.

She felt rotten. Sleeplessness and guilt made her queasy.

'The next few weeks will be frantic. You'll need to stay in top form. They want the pretty Princess, not the pale one,' King Giorgos turned back to the tablet he'd been staring at for the duration of the flight.

'Yes.'

She glanced out of the small window. Crowds had gathered with flags and celebratory signs. She quickly dug into her bag to do a touch-up on her blush, thankful that the jet had landed them back on Palisades.

Giorgos had escorted her on a three-day celebration visit of Santa Chiara to meet again with Prince Xander and his family. Not so long ago she'd have inwardly grimaced at her brother's smothering protectiveness, but she'd been glad of his presence. It had meant she'd not been left alone with Prince Xander.

The Shy Princess captures the Playboy Prince...

Their engagement had captured the imaginations of both nations. Her schedule and the resulting media interest had been beyond intense these last few weeks. At least all the appearances had kept her too busy to think. But late at night when she was alone in her private suite?

That was when she processed everything, reassuring herself she was safe. She would never tell anyone and that man from the ball would never tell anyone. He didn't even know who she was. She didn't know his name either. Only his face. Only his body.

She shivered but forced another smile when her brother glanced at her again. 'I'm going to go to my hospital visit this morning,' she said brightly.

Giorgos frowned. 'You don't wish to rest?'

Always protective. And also, always frowning.

She shook her head.

It had been nothing more than a sordid physical transaction. A ten-minute encounter between strangers. And surely, *please, please, please*, she would soon forget it. Because right now the memories were too real. She relived every moment, every word, every touch. And the worst thing? She wanted it again, wanted more, wanted it so much she burned with it. And then she burned with shame. Tears stung at the enormity of her betrayal. She was now engaged to another man yet all she could think of was *him*, that arrogant, intense stranger at the ball.

Thankfully displays of physical affection weren't 'done' between royals so the few 'kisses for the camera' on her tour with Prince Xander had been brief—her coolness read by the media as shyness. In private her fiancé had seemed happy to give her the time and space to adjust.

It was Giorgos who had asked if she was going to be happy with Xander and who'd reassured her that her fiancé's 'playboy' status was more media speculation than solid truth. For a moment she was tempted to confess her dreadful affair, but then she saw the tiredness in the back of her brother's eyes. He worked so hard for his people.

And she couldn't bear to see his crushing disappointment. She remembered how Giorgos had teased her with big-brother ruthlessness and laughter. But how he'd aged a decade overnight when their father died. Under the burden of all that responsibility he'd become serious, distant and more ruthless, without that humour. She understood he was wretchedly busy, but he'd tried his best for her—sending people to educate her, protect her, guide her. He just hadn't had the time himself. And she could not let him down.

He believed Xander to be the right fit for her—from a limited pool of options—and perhaps he was. So she'd make the best of it.

For Giorgos.

But the thought of her wedding night repulsed her. As crazy as it was, that brief conversation with that stranger at the ball had engendered far more trust in her than any of the discussions she'd had with polite, well-educated, aiming-to-please but ultimately careless Prince Xander. She simply didn't want him like that. She shivered again as that cold, sick feeling swept over her.

'I don't want to miss a visit,' she finally answered as she rose to disembark the jet.

She needed to do something slightly worthwhile because the guilt was eating her up. Her brother nodded and said nothing more. If anyone understood duty before all else, it was he.

An hour later, as she walked the corridor towards her favourite ward, that cold queasiness returned.

'Princess Eleni?' Kassie, the physiotherapist escorting her to the ward, stopped.

From a distance Eleni registered the woman was frowning and her voice sounded distanced too.

'Are you feeling okay?'

Damon Gale was barely existing in a state of perpetual anger. He hadn't left Palisades without trying to find and warn his mystery lover there might be consequences from their time together. He'd described her to his half-sister Kassie, but she'd not been able to identify the woman either. No one could. None of his subtle queries had given any answers. Where had she disappeared to so quickly? Heaven knew, when he found her he was giving her a piece of his mind. But at night she came to him in dream after dream.

He woke, hard, hungry and irritable as hell. There was so much more they should have done. But now she was hiding. Not least the truth about who she was. Why?

He loathed nothing more than lies.

So this morning, weeks since that damn ball, he'd once again flown back to Palisades. Now he waited for Kassie at the hospital in her tiny office, looking at the clever pen and ink drawings of the child patients pinned to the noticeboard.

He heard a footstep and a low, hurried whisper just outside the door.

'Ma'am, are you sure you're feeling all right?'

That was Kassie. Damon's muscles tensed.

'I'm just a bit…dizzy. Oh.' The woman groaned.

He froze, shocked at the second voice. He *knew* those raspy tones. She spoke in his dreams. Every. Damn. Night.

'Do you need a container?' Kassie asked delicately.

'I had a bug a few days ago but I thought I was over it or I'd never have visited today,' the woman muttered apologetically. 'I'm so sorry. I'd never want to put any of your patients at risk.'

'They're a hardy lot.' Now Kassie's smile was audible. 'I'm more concerned about you. Are you sure I can't get a doctor to check you over?'

'No, please. No fuss. I'll quickly go back to the palace. My driver is waiting.'

Palace? Damon was unable to move. Unable to speak. His woman had known the security code to get through that second door in the palace. Did she work there? But she'd said she worked at the hospital. That was why he was back here again.

'Maybe you should rest a moment,' Kassie urged softly.

'No. I need to go. I shouldn't have come.'

Damon stood. Those words exactly echoed ones he'd heard that night at the masked ball. Those exact tones in that exact, raspy voice. It was *her*.

He strode across the room and out into the corridor. But

his half-sister had her back to him and she was standing alone. Damon looked past her and saw no one—the corridor ended abruptly with a corner.

'Who was that?' he demanded harshly.

Kassie spun, startled. 'Damon?' She blinked at him. 'I didn't know you were coming back again so soon.'

'I have another meeting,' he clipped. 'Who were you talking to?'

'I'm not supposed to say because her visits are strictly private,' Kassie answered quietly. 'But she wasn't feeling well today and left early.'

'Whose visits?' What did she mean by 'private'?

'The Princess.'

Damon stared dumbfounded at his half-sister.

Princess Eleni of Palisades?

Wasn't she the younger sister of King Giorgos, a man known for his protectiveness and control over everything— his island nation, his emotions, his small *family*. Hadn't he been the guardian of the supposedly shy Princess for ever?

Now the covers of the newspapers at the airport flashed in his mind. He'd walked past them this morning but paid little attention because they'd all carried the same photo and same headline—

A Royal Engagement! The Perfect Prince for Our Princess!

But the Princess was not perfect. She'd fooled around with a total stranger only a few weeks ago. And now she was engaged. Had she been rebelling like some wilful teen? Or was there something more devious behind her shocking behaviour? And, heaven have mercy, how *old* was she?

'What do you think was wrong with her?' he asked Kassie uneasily. He needed to get alone and research more because an extremely bad feeling was building inside him.

'I'm not sure. She was pale and nau—'

'Where did she go?' he interrupted.

Kassie was staring at him. 'Back to the palace. She visits my ward every Friday. She never misses, no matter what.' Kassie ventured a small smile. 'She doesn't seem your type.'

He forced himself to answer idly, as if this didn't matter a jot. 'Do I have a type?'

Kassie's laugh held a nervous edge as she shook her head. 'Princess Eleni is very sweet and innocent.'

But that was where Kassie was wrong. Princess Eleni wasn't sweet or innocent at all. She was a liar and a cheat and he was going to tear her to shreds.

Thank God he finally knew where and how he could get to her. He just had to withstand waiting one more week.

CHAPTER FOUR

IN HER BATHROOM Eleni stared at her reflection. Her skin was leached of colour and she felt sick and tired all the time. Wretched nausea roiled in her stomach yet again, violent and irrepressible. She'd been avoiding mirrors since the ball. She couldn't see herself without seeing those two strangers entwined…

It had been over a month since that night. Now she gazed at her breasts and held in her agonised gasp. Was it her imagination or were they fuller than usual? That would be because her period was due, right? But finally she made herself face the fact she'd been trying desperately to forget. Her period was more than due. It was late.

Two weeks late.

She'd been busy. She'd been travelling. Her cycle could be screwed up by nerves, couldn't it?

Frigid fear slithered down her spine as bitter acid flooded her mouth again. Because a lone, truly terrifying reason for her recurring sickness gripped her.

Surely it was impossible. She'd seen him put on that condom. She couldn't possibly be pregnant. That foul acid burned its way up into her mouth. She closed her eyes as tears stung and then streamed down her face. She needed help and she needed it now.

But there was no help to be had. She had no true friends to trust. Her childhood companions had been carefully selected for their families' loyalty to the crown and swiftly excised from her life if they'd slightly transgressed. There were acquaintances but no real confidantes and now most were in continental Europe getting on with their careers.

Eleni had studied at home. It was 'safer'; it endorsed

their own, prestigious university; it was what Giorgos had wanted. She'd not argued, not wanting to cause him trouble.

She was terrified of troubling him now.

But she was going to have to. Shaking, she showered then dressed. She quickly typed an email to Giorgos's secretary requesting a meeting for this evening. Her brother was busy, but Prince Xander was arriving from Santa Chiara tonight for a week's holiday with her. They'd be travelling to the outer islands to spend more time together. She was dreading it. She had to speak to Giorgos first. She had to tell him the truth.

Still incredibly cold, she grabbed a jacket and stuffed a cap in the pocket while her maid, Bettina, phoned for her car.

It was far later than when she usually went to the hospital, but she was desperate to get away from her suite where her maid was lining up sample wedding dresses from the world's top designers. The only thing she could do while waiting to meet Giorgos was maintain some kind of schedule. Given she'd left her visit so abruptly last week, she couldn't miss this week as well. She'd control the nausea and control her life.

Once she got to the hospital she asked Tony, her security detail, to wait for her outside. But she didn't go into the ward, and instead walked along the corridor to the other side of the building. She tugged on the cap and headed out to the private hospital garden. She needed to steel herself for the polite questions from the patients she'd come to help entertain. But she'd been lying all day, every day for the last few weeks and it was taking its toll. Telling people over and over again how excited she was at the prospect of marrying Prince Xander was exhausting. And horrible. But the bigger the lie, the more believable it apparently was.

She leaned over the wrought-iron railing, looking down at the river. She was going to have to go back and front up to Giorgos. Her gut churned, but it wasn't the pregnancy hormones making her nauseous now. How did she admit this all to him?

I'm sorry. I'm so sorry.

Sorry wasn't going to be good enough. She dreaded sinking so low in his eyes. Never had she regretted anything as much as her recklessness that night at the ball.

A prickle of awareness pressed on her spine—intuition whispered she was no longer alone. Warily she turned away from the water.

'You okay?' The man stood only a couple of paces away. 'Or are you feeling a little blue?'

The bitterness in that soft-spoken query devastated her. It was *him.* Her blood rushed and the edges of her vision blackened as she shrank back. Something grasped her elbow tightly, the pain pulling her from the brink of darkness.

'It's okay, I'm not going to let you fall.'

He was there and he was too close, with his words in her ear and his strength in his grip and his heat magnetic.

Oh, no. No.

'I'm sorry.' Eleni ignored the sweat suddenly slithering down her spine and snapped herself together.

He released her the second she tugged her arm back, but he didn't step away. So he was close. Too close.

'I don't know what came over me.' She leaned against the railing, unable to stop the trembling of her legs or the jerkiness of her breathing.

'Yeah, you do.' He leaned against the wrought iron too, resting his hand on the rail between them. Not relaxed. *Ready to strike.*

Tall, dark and dangerous, he looked like some streetwise power player in his black trousers, black jersey, aviator sunglasses and unreadable expression.

'There's no point trying to hide any more, Eleni,' he

said. 'I know who you are and I know exactly what your problem is.'

She froze. 'I don't have a problem.'

'Yeah, you do. You and I created it together. Now we're going to resolve it. Together.'

All strength vanished from her legs. They'd *created* it? The full horror hit as she realised he *knew*.

'I'm sorry,' she repeated mechanically. 'I don't know who you are and I don't know what you're talking about.' She willed her strength back. 'If you'll forgive me, I need to go.'

'No.' He removed his sunglasses. 'I won't forgive you.'

Her heart stuttered at the emotion reflected in his intense blue eyes. Accusation. Betrayal. Anger...and something else.

Something she dared not try to define.

She clenched her fists and plunged them into the pockets of her jacket, fighting the paralysis. 'I have to leave.'

'Not this time. You're coming with me, Eleni. You know we need to talk.'

'I can't do that.' Why had she thought it wise not to tell her security detail where she was going?

'Yes, you can. Because if you don't...'

'What?' She drew in a sharp breath as a sense of fatality struck. 'What will you do?'

Of course it would come to an ultimatum. The determination had been on his face from the second she'd seen him. He was livid.

'You come with me now and we take the time to sort this out, or I tell the world you're pregnant from screwing a stranger at the palace ball.'

His tawdry description of what they'd done stabbed. It hadn't been a 'screw'. It had meant more than she could ever admit to anyone.

'No one would believe you,' she muttered.

'You're *that* good at lying?' He was beyond livid. 'You

want this scandal dragged through the press? That you're going to marry a man without telling him that you're pregnant, most probably by another?'

She flinched at his cruelly blunt words but she latched onto the realisation that he wasn't *sure* the baby was his.

'You want the whole world to know that you're not the perfect Princess after all?' he goaded her relentlessly. 'But a liar and a cheater?'

'I've never been the perfect Princess,' she snapped back, defensive and hurt and unable to stay calm a second longer.

'Come on.' The softness of his swift reply stunned her.

Her heart thundered. He'd echoed the forbidden words from weeks ago. Heat flared. So wrong.

'I can't,' she reminded him—and herself—through gritted teeth. 'My fiancé is arriving in Palisades tonight.'

'Really?' He glared at her. 'That cheating life is what you really want?' His frustration seeped through. 'That's why you're standing by the river looking like you're about to throw yourself in? You're lost, Eleni.'

'You don't know what I am.'

He knew nothing about her and she knew as little about him—not even his damn name.

Except that wasn't quite true. She knew more important things—his determination, his strength, his consideration.

And *her* guilt.

'The one thing I do know is that you're pregnant and the baby very well might be mine. You owe me a conversation at least.'

He wasn't going anywhere and he was perfectly capable of acting on his threat, she knew that about him too. She tried to regain her customary calm, and decided to bluff. 'So talk.'

'Somewhere private.' He glanced up at the multi-storeyed hospital building behind her. 'Where we can't be seen or overheard.'

That made sense but it was impossible. She shook her head.

'My car is just around the corner,' he said, unconcerned at her latest refusal.

Her heart thudded. She shouldn't go anywhere alone with any man and certainly not this one.

'I'll go straight to the media,' he promised coolly. 'And I have proof. I still have your underwear.'

She was aghast; her jaw dropped.

'You *wouldn't*,' she choked.

'I'm prepared to do whatever is necessary to get this sorted out,' he replied blandly, putting his sunglasses back on. 'I suggest you walk with me now.'

What choice did she have?

She hardly saw where she was going as she moved back through the hospital, then to the right instead of the left. Away from her guard. Hopefully Tony wouldn't notice for a few minutes yet—in all her life she'd never caused trouble for him.

She slid into the passenger seat of his car.

'Five minutes,' she said just as he closed the door for her.

He was still laughing, bitterly, as he got in, locked the doors and started the engine. 'You might want to put on your seat belt, because it's going to take a little longer than that this time, sweetheart.' He pulled out into the road. 'We have a lifetime to work out.'

'Where are you taking me?' She broke into a cold sweat.

'As I said, somewhere private. Somewhere where we won't be disturbed.'

'You can't take me away from here.' Frantically she twisted in her seat, terrified to see the hospital getting smaller as they moved away from it.

'I know how quickly you can move, Eleni. I'm not taking the risk of you running from me this time.'

Surprised, she turned to face him.

'Relax.' He sent her an ironic glance. 'I'm not going to hurt you, Princess. We just need to talk.'

Sure, she knew he wouldn't hurt her physically. But in other ways? She tried to clear her head. 'You have the better of me. I don't even know your name.'

'So you're finally curious enough to ask?' His hands tightened on the steering wheel. 'My name is Damon Gale. I'm the CEO of a tech company that specialises in augmented reality. I have another company that's working on robotics. Most women think I'm something of a catch.'

Damon. Crisp and masculine. It suited him.

'I'm not like most women.' She prickled at his arrogance. 'And a lot of men think I'm a catch.'

'You definitely took some catching,' he murmured, pulling into a car park and killing the engine. 'Yet here we are.'

Eleni looked out of the car window and saw he meant literally. He'd brought her to the marina. 'Why are we here?'

'I need the certainty that you won't do one of your disappearing acts, but we can't have this argument in the front seat of a car and...' He hesitated as he stared at her. 'We need space.'

Space? Eleni's heart thundered as she gazed into his eyes. Beneath her shock and fear something else stirred—awareness, recognition.

This is the one I had. This is the one I want.

Suddenly that forbidden passion pulsed through every fibre of her being.

Unbidden. Unwanted. Undeniable.

CHAPTER FIVE

HE'D KNOWN HER eyes weren't that unnaturally intense
indigo they'd been at the ball, but the discovery of their
true colour had stolen a breath that Damon still hadn't recovered. They were sea green—a myriad of bewitching
shades—and he couldn't summon the strength to look away.

She lies.

He reminded himself. Again.

The alluring Princess Eleni Nicolaides had used him
and he couldn't possibly be considering kissing her. He'd
not been completely certain before but he was now—she
was pregnant. To him.

Grimly he shoved himself out of the car and stalked
around it to open her door. Impatiently he watched the emotions flicker across her too-expressive face—wariness, cu-
riosity, decision—and beneath those? Desire.

His body tightened. More than anger, this was possessiveness. So off-base. Rigid with self-control, he took her
arm, steeling himself not to respond to the electricity that
surged between them. It took only a minute to guide her
down the steps and along the wooden landing to his yacht.
She stopped and stared at it.

'Eleni,' he prompted her curtly. 'We need to talk.'

'You have to take me back soon.' She twisted her hands
together. 'They'll be wondering where I am.'

'They can wonder for a while yet,' he muttered.

He hustled her past the cabin and through to the lounge.
The windows were tinted so no one on deck could see them,
and his sparse crew were under strict instruction to stay out
of sight and work quickly. He remained in front of the only
exit to the room. He couldn't be careful enough with her.

'Take off the cap.' He could hardly push the words past the burr in his throat, but he needed to see her with no damn disguise.

She lifted the cap. Her hair wasn't long and blue, it was cut to a length just below her chin and was blonde—corn silk soft, all natural and, right now, tousled.

'How did you figure out who I was?' she asked in that damnably raspy voice.

He shook his head.

Once he'd realised who his mystery lover was, he'd been lame enough to look online. But she was more perfect in the flesh. Tall and slender, strong and feminine, with those curves that caused the most base reaction in him. Her complexion was flawless and her sweetheart-shaped face captivating. But her beauty was a façade that apparently masked a shockingly salacious soul. He was determined to get to the truth.

'You knew I was going to be at the hospital,' she said after he didn't reply to her first question. 'How?'

Her fingers trembled as she fidgeted with the cap, but he'd not brought her here to answer *her* questions.

'Were you going to tell him?' he asked.

He glared as she didn't answer. She was so good at avoiding everything important, wasn't she?

He felt the vibration beneath the deck as the engines fired up. About time. Icily satisfied, he silently kept watching. Now she'd be tested. Sure enough, as the yacht moved she strode to the window.

'Where are you taking me?' she asked, her volume rising.

'Somewhere private.' Somewhere isolated. Triumph rushed at the prospect of having her completely alone.

'This *is* private. We don't need to move to make it more so.' Panic filled her voice and turned wide eyes on him. 'This is abduction.'

'Is it?' he asked, uncaring. 'But you agreed to come with me.'

'I didn't realise you meant…' She paled. 'I can't just *leave.*'

He hardened his heart. 'Why not? You've done that before.'

This was the woman who'd had sex with him when she knew she was about to announce her engagement to another man. Who'd then run off without another word. And who was now pregnant and concealing it—apparently from everyone.

The betrayal burned like no other. He hated being *used.* His father had used him as cover for his long-term infidelities. His mother had used his entire existence to promote her political aspirations—hell, she'd even told him she never would have had him if it weren't for the possible benefit to her career. His father had not only agreed, he'd expected Damon to understand and become the same. A parasite—using anyone and anything to enhance success. He'd refused and he'd vowed that he'd never let anyone use him again.

But Eleni had.

Yet that look on her face now was torture—those shimmering eyes, the quiver of her full lips.

Desire tore through his self-control, forcing him closer to her. Furious, he locked it down, viciously clenching his fists and shoving them into his trouser pockets. It was this uncontrolled lust that had got him into this mess in the first place.

It was insane. Once more he reminded himself he knew nothing of importance about her other than her shocking ability to conceal information. But as he watched, she whitened further. Whitened to the point of—

'Eleni?' He rushed forward.

'Oh, hell.' She pressed her hand to her mouth.

Oh, hell was right. He reached for a decorative bowl just in time.

***

Oh, no. No.

Eleni groaned but the sickness couldn't be stopped. Of all the mortifying things to happen.

'Sit down before you fall down,' he muttered.

'I'm not used to being on the water,' she replied.

'If you're going to lie, at least try to make it believable. It's well known you love sailing, Princess. Your illness is caused by your pregnancy.'

She was too queasy to bother trying to contradict him. What was the point? 'I need fresh air.'

'You need to stay in here until we're away from the island.'

'You can't be serious.' Aghast, she stared up at him. 'You're going to cause an international incident.'

'Do you think so?' He stared at her grimly. 'I think the spectacle is only going to get even more insane when they find out I'm the father of your unborn child.'

She closed her eyes and groaned. 'At least let me use a bathroom.'

'Of course.'

He guided her to a small room. He opened a drawer and handed her a toothbrush, still in its packet. She took it, silently grateful as he left her in privacy.

But he was just outside the door when she opened it again a few minutes later.

She walked back into the lounge just as a uniformed crew member was leaving. The man didn't say a word, didn't meet her eyes. He simply melted from the room.

'Who was that?' she asked.

'Someone extremely discreet and very well paid.'

He'd left fresh water in a tall glass and a few crackers on a plate. She turned away; there was no way she could eat anything right now.

'You're naive if you think he won't sell your secrets.'

The man had recognised her. It was only a matter of time before people came to her rescue.

'I've been betrayed before, Eleni. I know how to make my business safe.'

Eleni looked at the hard edge of Damon's jaw and wondered who had betrayed him. 'Your business?'

'My baby.'

Her blood chilled. 'So you planned this.'

There'd been a crew ready and waiting on this boat and no doubt he paid them ridiculously well. He'd gone to huge trouble to get her away from the palace. Maybe she ought to feel scared, she barely knew him after all, but she didn't believe she was in danger. Rather, in that second, the craziest feeling bloomed in her chest.

Relief.

His eyes narrowed. 'You know this isn't about rescuing you.'

His words hit like bullets. She shrank, horrified that he'd seen her *selfishness*. Guilt brought defensiveness with it. 'I don't need rescuing.'

His smile mocked. 'No?'

Damon was more dangerous than she'd realised. She couldn't cope with her reaction to him. It was as if everything else in the world, everything that mattered, simply evaporated in his presence. His pull was too strong.

But then she remembered he wasn't certain she was pregnant to *him*. Perhaps her way out was to convince him he *wasn't* the father. Then he'd return her to Palisades. She'd go to Giorgos. She should have gone to Giorgos already.

'I *can't* stay here,' she pleaded.

'Give in, Eleni,' he replied indifferently. 'You already are. The question is, can you be honest?'

Not with him. Not now.

But she burned to prove that she didn't need 'rescuing'—not from her situation, or from herself. He strolled towards her but she wasn't fooled by the ease of his movement. He was furious. Well, that made two of them.

'How many other possibilities are there?' he asked too softly, his gaze penetrating.

'Excuse me?' She tensed as he came within touching distance.

'Who are the other men who might be the father of your child?' He watched her so intently she feared he could see every hidden thought, every contrary emotion.

'Can you even remember them all?' he challenged.

She flushed at his tone, lost for words.

'You have sex with me at a ball within five minutes of meeting me,' he murmured, continuing his hateful judgment. 'You didn't even know my name.'

'And you didn't know mine,' she flared. 'And we used protection. So there you go.'

'But *I* wasn't engaged to anyone else at the time.'

That one hurt because it was truth. 'Nor was I,' she mumbled weakly.

'Not "officially".' His eyes were so full of scorn that she winced. 'But you *knew*. You knew the announcement was about to be made. You owed him your loyalty and you cheated.'

Damon was right, but he didn't know the reality of the marriage she faced. He'd never understand the scrutiny and crazy constraints she endured in her privileged world.

At her silence now, pure danger flashed in his eyes. She backed away until the wall brought her to a stop. Her heart raced as he followed until he leaned right into her personal space.

'So, how many others?' he asked again, too softly.

She'd brazen it out. Disgust him so he'd take her back to Palisades in repulsion. 'At least four.'

'Liar.' Slowly he lifted his hand and brushed the backs of his fingers over the blush burning down her cheekbones. 'Why won't you just tell me the truth, Eleni?'

His whisper was so tempting.

She lifted her chin, refusing to let him seduce her again. And at the same time, refusing to run. 'I don't have to tell you anything.'

'What are you afraid of?' he taunted huskily. 'The world finding out your secret? That Princess Eleni The Pure likes dressing up in disguise and doing it fast and dirty with a succession of strangers? That she can't get enough?'

Anger ignited, but something else was lit within as well. That treacherous response. She *had* liked it fast and dirty. With him. She closed her eyes but he tilted her chin back up, holding it until she opened them again and looked right into the banked heat of his.

'Are you ashamed of what happened, Eleni?'

Tears stung but she blinked them back. Of *course* she was ashamed. She couldn't understand how it had happened. How she could have lost all control and all reason like that. And how could her body be so traitorous now— aching for him to take that half step nearer and touch her again?

The intensity deepened in his eyes. A matching colour mounted in his cheekbones.

Hormones. Chemicals. That crazy reaction that she still couldn't believe had happened was happening again.

'You like it,' he muttered. 'And you want it.'

'And I get it,' she spat, reckless and furious and desperate to push him away. 'From whomever, whenever I please.'

'Is that right?'

'Yes,' she slammed her answer in defiance.

He smiled. A wickedly seductive smile of utter disbelief.

'You'll never know.' She was pushed to scorn.

'You don't think?' He actually laughed.

'Maybe I'm pregnant with my fiancé's baby,' she snapped. Reminding him of her engagement might make him back off. She *needed* him to back off.

His smile vanished. 'I don't think so, Princess.'

She stilled at his expression.

'You haven't slept with him,' Damon said roughly. 'I was your first, Eleni. That night with me, you were a virgin.'

She gaped, floundering in total mortification as he threw the truth in her face.

How had he known? How? She pressed against the cool wall, hoping to stop shaking.

'Why lie so constantly?' he demanded, leaning closer, the heat of his body blasting. 'You still have nothing to say?'

How could she possibly explain? She couldn't answer even her own conscience.

'There is nothing wrong with liking sex,' he said roughly. 'But there is something wrong with lying and cheating to get it.'

She trembled again, appalled by how aroused she was. She could no longer look him in the eye; he saw too much. She wanted to hide from him. From herself. Since when was she this wanton animal who'd forgo all her scruples simply to get a physical fix?

'Eleni.'

She refused to look at him.

But she couldn't escape the sensations that the slightest of touches summoned. He brushed her cheek with a single finger, and then tucked a strand of her hair back behind her ear. She stood rigid, desperate not to reveal any reaction.

'Let's try this again, shall we?' He leaned so close.

She bit the inside of her cheek, hoping the pain would help keep her sane, but she could feel his heat radiating through her.

'No lying. No cheating,' he murmured. 'Just truth.'

The tip of his finger marauded back and forth over her lips; the small caress sent shock waves of sensuality to her most private depths.

Her pulse quickened, but his finger didn't. Slowly he teased. Such pleasure and such promise came from a touch so small, building until she could no longer hold still. He teased until she parted her lips with a shaky breath.

He swooped, pressing his mouth to hers, taking advantage to slide his tongue deep and taste until he tore a soft moan from her. So easily. He wound his arm around her waist and drew her close, holding her so he could kiss her. Again. Then again.

After all these sleepless nights he was with her—with all his heat and hardness. She quivered, then melted against him. Immediately he swept his hand down her side, urging her closer and she went—her body softening to accommodate the steel of his.

With his hands and with his lips, he marauded everywhere now. Kissing her mouth, her jaw, her neck, he slid his hand across her aching breasts, down her quivering stomach, until he hit the hem of her skirt. He pushed under and up. High, then higher still up her thigh. Demanding—and getting—acceptance, intimacy, willingness. So quickly. So intensely. She curled into his embrace, then arched taut as a bowstring as he teased her.

'Eleni...' he whispered between kisses and caresses. 'How many lovers have you had?'

Unable to contain her need, she thrust against that tormenting finger that was so close, that was stirring her in a way that she could no longer resist. On a desperate sigh she finally surrendered her not so secret truth. 'One.'

He rewarded her with more of that rubbing designed to drive her insane. She couldn't breathe. Closer, *so* close.

'And how many times have you had sex?'

She shook with aching desire. With the need for him to touch her again. Just once. One more touch was all she needed. 'One,' she muttered breathlessly.

Her answer seemed to anger him again. He held her fast and kissed her hard. Passionate and ruthless, his tongue plundered the cavern of her mouth. He was dominant and claiming and all she could do was yield to his passion.

But the fires within him stoked her own. She kissed him back furiously, hating him knowing how aroused she was. But there was no controlling her reaction. No stopping what she wanted. And she *wanted. Now.*

It was at that moment, of her total surrender, that he tore his mouth from hers.

'How many men have kissed you like that?' he rasped.

She panted, her nipples tight and straining against her suddenly too tight bra. *'One,'* she answered, pushed beyond her limits.

'And how many men have kissed you liked that, but *here*?' His fingers pushed past the silk scrap of material covering her, probing into her damp, hot sex.

She gasped at the delicious intrusion. Her limbs trembled as release hovered only a stroke or two away. She gazed into his gorgeously fiery eyes, quivering at the extreme intimacy connecting them.

'Answer me, Eleni.' He ground out a brutal whisper.

'None.' Her answer barely sounded.

She registered his sharp exhalation but then he kissed her again. Somehow she was in his embrace, his body between hers. Heaven help her, she went with him to that sofa. She let him. Wanted him. But as he pushed her skirt higher and slid lower so he was kneeling between her legs she realised where this was going. A lucid moment—she gasped and shifted.

'Don't try to hide. I'm going to kiss you. There won't be even an inch of you that I haven't tasted. Every intimacy is *mine*.'

His blunt, savage words stunned her. Blindly she realised that his control was as splintered as her own. That he too was pushed beyond reason. Pleasure surged and she couldn't resist or deny—not him. Not herself.

She groaned at his first kiss, shocked at how exposed she felt and embarrassed by just how much she ached for his touch. It was like being taken over by a part of herself she didn't know was there. That lustful, brazen part. She flung her arm over her face, hiding from him. From herself. But there was no hiding from the sensations he aroused and the delight and skill of his mouth on her. His tongue. There. Right there.

She moaned in unspeakable pleasure.

'Look at that,' he muttered arrogantly in the echo of her need. 'You like it.' His laugh was exultant. 'You like it a lot.'

His attention was relentless. She arched again, pressing her hands against her eyes but unable to hold back her scream as a torrent of ecstasy tore through her. She shuddered, sweet torture wracking her body.

Then she was silent, suspended in that moment where she waited for his next move. For him to rise above her, to press against her, to take her. She ached anew to feel him. She wanted him to push inside and take her completely.

But he didn't. He didn't move at all.

She lay frozen, her face still buried in her arm as the last vestiges of that bliss ebbed. And then shame flooded in. Bitter, galling shame.

She twisted, suddenly desperate to escape. But he grasped her hips hard, prevented her moving even an inch.

'Stop hiding,' he growled savagely. 'There are things we must discuss.'

'Discuss? You think you discuss anything?' She threw her arms wide and snarled at him. 'You dictate.' He *bulldozed*. 'And you…you…'

'Take action.' He finished her sentence for her, as breathless and angry as she. 'And I'll continue to do so. And first up, you're not going to marry Prince Xander of Santa Chiara. You're going to marry me.'

CHAPTER SIX

'I'M NOT MARRYING YOU,' Eleni snapped, furiously shoving him. 'I'm not marrying anyone.'

'Right.' He lazily leaned back on his heels and sent her a sardonic look. 'That's why the world is currently planning party snacks for the live stream of the royal wedding of the century.'

She was sick of his smug arrogance. Awkwardly she curled up her legs to get past him and angrily pulled her skirt down, too mortified to hunt for her knickers. 'I wasn't going to go through with it.'

'Really?' He stood in a single, smooth movement, mocking her with his athletic grace. 'What was the plan?'

She loathed how inept he made her feel. How easily he could make her lose all control. How much her appallingly stupid body still wanted his attention. 'You have no idea how impossible it is for me to get away.'

'As it happens, I do have some insight into the technical difficulties.' His gaze narrowed. Hardened. 'So you were going to go through with it.'

She'd never wanted to but she'd known it was what was expected. Since she'd suspected her pregnancy her desperation had grown. She glared at him from the centre of the room. 'I didn't know what to do.'

'Why not try talking to him?'

She rolled her eyes. He made it sound so easy.

'Giorgos wouldn't listen.'

'Giorgos?' Damon's eyebrows shot up. 'What about the man you were supposed to marry?'

Who? Oh. He meant Xander. As if she could talk to him—she barely knew him.

'I'm guessing you don't love him. Prince Xander, that is,' Damon added sarcastically.

She turned away from Damon. Her heart beat heavy and fast and she perched on the edge of a small chair—far, far away from that sofa. 'Obviously not or I wouldn't have... done what I did with you.'

'Then why marry him?'

'Because it is what has been expected for a long time.'

'So it's duty.'

'It would benefit our countries...'

'Because a royal wedding is somehow going to magically smooth away any serious issues your respective countries may be facing?' He laughed derisively. 'And you'll throw in some rainbows and unicorns to make it all prettier and perfect?'

'You don't understand the subtleties.'

'Clearly not,' he muttered dryly. 'And was my child meant to be the fruit of this fairy-tale unity?' he demanded. 'When in reality she or he will grow up lonely in a house devoid of warmth and love with parents absent in every sense.'

Eleni stared, taken aback by his vehemence. And his insight.

'I'll never let my child be used that way.' His eyes were hard. 'I know the unseen impact of a purely political union and I'll do whatever it takes to ensure my kid doesn't endure that kind of bleak upbringing.'

'I'm not going to marry him,' she said in a low voice. 'I know I can't.'

'But if you don't marry someone, your child will be labelled a bastard. We might live in modern times, but you're a *princess* and there are certain expectations. What kind of life will your child have without legitimacy? Will she be kept cloistered in the shadows, even more stifled than you were? Look how well that turned out for you.'

She flinched. He saw too much and he judged harshly.

But the horrible thing was, he was right. She had to think of a better way. She leapt to her feet and paced away from him, twisting her cold hands together. She didn't want to involve *him*—he twisted everything up too much.

'I need to call Giorgos,' she said. It must be almost two hours since she'd left Palisades and her brother would be irate already.

'I agree.'

She spun on the spot. 'You do?'

'Of course. It'll be better if you're completely honest with him. Do you think you can be—or are you going to need help with that again?'

She flushed, remembering just how Damon had dragged the intimate truth from her only minutes ago. Now his biting sarcasm hurt and she felt sick enough at the thought of confessing all to her brother.

'What, you expect me to cheerily tell him I'm here of my own free will?' She flared. 'That you didn't bundle me into a boat and set sail for the high seas before I could blink?'

'The choice was yours.'

'What choice did you give me?' she scoffed.

'To speak the truth, or give you time. I think it was a reasonable choice.'

'It was blackmail. Because you're a bully.'

'You've already admitted you didn't know what to do. You couldn't figure a way out. Here it is and you're happy about it. Don't dramatise me into your villain.'

Eleni rubbed her forehead. Damon's words struck a deep chord. She'd been refusing to admit to herself how glad she was he'd stolen her away. She'd been unable to think up an escape and he'd offered one. She wasn't as much mad with him, but mad with herself for needing it—and for layering on complications with her wretched desire for him. Her emotional overreactions had to end.

She'd been too scared to admit to Giorgos how badly

she'd screwed up. But if she wanted her brother to treat her as an adult, she had to act like one.

'Okay.' She blew out a breath and turned to look Damon in the eye. 'I'm not sorry you took me away. You're right. I needed this time to think things through. Thank you.'

'How very gracious, Princess,' Damon drawled. 'But don't be mistaken. Like I said, this isn't a rescue. I'm not doing you a favour. I'm claiming what's mine. And I'm protecting it.' He picked up a handset from a small side table and held it out to her. 'Phone your brother.'

Eleni's hands were slick with sweat as she tapped the private number onto the screen.

'Giorgos, it's me.' She turned away from Damon as her brother answered his private line immediately.

'Eleni. Where are you?' Giorgos demanded instant answers. 'Come back to the palace now. Do you have any idea of the trouble you've caused?'

'I'm not coming back yet, Giorgos. I need time to think.'

'Think? About what?' Her brother dismissed her claim. 'Your fiancé is already here. Or had you forgotten that you're about to go on tour with him?'

'I can't do it, Giorgos.'

'Can't do what?' Giorgos asked impatiently.

Eleni closed her eyes and summoned all her courage. 'I'm pregnant,' she said flatly. 'Prince Xander isn't the father.'

Silence.

Seven long seconds of appalled silence.

'Who?' Giorgos finally asked in a deadly whisper. *'Who?'*

'It doesn't matter—'

'I'll kill him. I'll bloody— Tell me his name.'

'No.'

'Tell me his name, Eleni. I'll have him—'

'Call off the hounds, Giorgos.' She interrupted her brother for the first time in her life. 'Or I swear I'll never return.' Her heart broke as she threatened him. 'I will disappear.'

Her guilt mounted. Her horror at doing this to the brother she loved. But she pushed forward.

'It doesn't matter who it was. He didn't seduce me. I was a fully willing participant.' She screwed her eyes tight shut, mortified at revealing this intimacy to her brother, but knowing the way he'd assume she'd been taken advantage of because he still thought of her as an innocent, helpless kid. She needed to *own* this. 'I made the mistake, Giorgos. And I need to fix it. Tell Xander I'm sick. Tell him I ran away. Tell him anything you like. But I'm not coming back. Not yet. Not 'til I've sorted it out.'

'Are you with the bastard now?' Giorgos asked impatiently.

'I'm not marrying him either,' Eleni said.

She didn't catch Giorgos's muttered imprecation.

'This child is mine. Pure Nicolaides.' She finally felt a segment of peace settle in place inside.

This was what she should have done at the beginning. She had to make amends now—to all the people she'd involved. 'And please don't blame Tony for losing track of me. It wasn't his fault.'

'Your protection officer has no idea where you've gone. He's clearly incompetent. He has been dismissed.'

'But it's not his fault.' Eleni's voice rose. Tony had been with Eleni for years. He had a wife and two children. He needed the work. 'I told him—'

'Lies,' Giorgos snapped. 'But it *is* his fault that he lost track of you. His employment is not your concern.'

'But—'

'You should have thought through the consequences of your actions, Eleni. There are ramifications for *all* the people of Palisades. And Santa Chiara.'

Twin tears slid out from her closed eyes. She would make it up to Tony somehow. Another atonement to be made.

'How do I stop a scandal here, Eleni?' Giorgos asked.

She cringed. Was that what mattered most—the reputation of the royal family? But she knew that was unfair to Giorgos. He was trying to protect *her*. It was what he'd always done. Too much.

'I'm so sorry,' she said dully. 'I take full responsibility. I will be in touch when I can.'

She ended the call before her brother could berate her any more. She turned and saw Damon casually leaning against the back of the sofa as if he were watching a mildly entertaining movie.

'Did you have to listen in?' Angered, she wiped the tears away. 'You know they'll have traced the call.'

'And they'll find it leads to some isolated shack in Estonia.' He shrugged. 'I work in the tech industry, Eleni. They won't find us in the next few days, I promise you that. We're hidden and we're safe.'

'What, this is some superhero space boat that can engage stealth mode?' She shook her head. 'They'll be checking the coastline.'

'And we're already miles away from it and your brother knows you're not under duress. You've shocked him, Eleni. I'm sure he'll wait to hear from you. The last thing he'll want now is the publicity from mounting a full-scale search and rescue operation.'

She'd shocked Giorgos. Once he'd got past that, the disappointment would zoom in. She was glad she wasn't there to see it.

'There's one option we haven't talked about,' Damon said expressionlessly. 'It is early enough in the pregnancy for termination to be—'

'No,' she interrupted him vehemently.

She had such privilege. She had money. This child could be well cared for.

And it was *hers*.

That was the thing. For the first time in her life she had

something that was truly, utterly her own. Her responsibility. Her concern. Hers to love and protect. No one was taking it away from her. There was a way out of this if she was strong enough to stand up to her brother's—and her nation's—disappointment. And she was determined to be.

'I'm not marrying Prince Xander,' she said fiercely. 'I'm not marrying you. I'm not marrying anyone. But I *am* having this baby.' She pulled herself together—*finally* feeling strong. 'I have the means and the wherewithal to provide for my baby on my own. And that is what I will do.'

'Do you?' Damon looked sceptical. 'What if Giorgos cuts you off completely? How will you fend for yourself then?'

'He wouldn't do that.' Her brother would be beyond disappointed, but he wouldn't abandon her. She should have trusted him more, sooner.

'Even so, what price will you pay for one moment of recklessness?' Damon badgered. 'The rest of your life in disgrace.'

'I could step away from the spotlight and live in one of the remote villages.' She would ask for nothing from the public purse.

It was the personal price that pained her. She'd let her brother down in both public and private senses. But she would not let this baby down. She'd made her first stand, and now she had to follow through and not let Damon block her way either.

'So that's your escape neatly done,' he noted softly. 'But what price will my *child* pay if you do that?'

She flushed, unsettled by his cool sarcasm. He made it sound as if she was thinking only of herself, not her baby. But she wasn't. She'd understood what he'd said about a child growing up with all that expectation and wasn't this a way of removing that?

But he clearly considered that she'd been stifled and cloistered and, yes, spoilt. He thought her behaviour with him at the ball a direct consequence of that. Maybe he was right. That flush deepened. She loathed this man.

'I'm not marrying you,' she repeated. She *couldn't*.

The absolute last thing Damon Gale wanted to do was marry—her or anyone—but damn if her rejection didn't just irritate the hell out of him. What, was his billionaire bank balance not good enough for her spoilt royal self?

He'd sworn never to engage in even a 'serious' relationship. But the worst of all possible options was a 'politically expedient' wedding. Yet now he was insulted because, while she'd agreed to a political marriage once already, she was adamantly refusing his offer. Why? Because he wasn't a *prince*?

'I'll never let you use my baby for your political machinations.' He glared at her.

All she did was stick her chin in the air and glare back.

His body burned and he paced away from her. That damned sexual ache refused to ease. Heaven only knew why he wanted this woman. But it had been like this since the moment he'd first seen her at that ball. To his immense satisfaction, he'd had her—there and then. He'd immediately wanted more, but then she'd fled.

Now he'd finally found her again, yet within moments of getting her alone on his boat he'd totally lost control and done exactly what he'd promised himself he wouldn't. He'd touched her. Instead of verbally tearing her to shreds, he'd pressed his mouth to her until she'd warmed like wax in his hands. Pliable and willing and ultimately so wanton and gorgeous. It had taken every speck of self-control to not claim her completely there on the sofa.

He knew he could use this mutual lust to get the acquiescence to his proposal he needed, but he wanted more than her gasping surrender. He wanted her to accept that he was *right*. Poor little princess was going to have to marry a mere man. A man she wanted in spite of herself, apparently.

'What were you thinking at that ball?' He couldn't understand why she'd taken such a massive risk. Was it just lust for her too or had there been more to it? Had she been trying to sabotage that engagement? But to throw away her virginity?

'Clearly I wasn't. What were *you* thinking?'

He leaned back against the wall. He'd been thinking how beautiful she was. How something vulnerable in her had pulled him to her.

'I tried to find you because I realised the condom had torn, but you'd vanished from the ball like a—' He broke off. 'I was on a flight the next day. I came back several times, but couldn't find any information about you. I asked—'

'You asked?'

'Everyone I knew. No one had seen you there. You never went back into the ballroom.' He shook his head and asked again. 'Why did you do it?'

Her shoulders lifted in a helpless shrug.

He hesitated but in the end was unable to stop the words coming out. 'Did you even think of trying to get in touch with me?'

Her beautiful face paled. 'I didn't know your name. I wasn't about to run a search on all the guys who'd been at that ball. I couldn't risk anyone suspecting me. How could I tell anyone?'

'How hard would it have been to go through that guest list?' he asked irritably. 'To identify men between a certain age? To look at security footage? You could easily have found out who I was, Eleni. You just didn't want to.' And that annoyed him so much more than it should.

'If I'd tried to do that, people would have asked *why*.'

'And you didn't want them to do that, because you'd already made a promise to another man.' He ran his hand through his hair in frustration. 'I've seen those "official" photos. They weren't taken the day after you slept with me. They were taken before, weren't they?'

She couldn't look him in the eye. 'Yes.'

Damon's blood pressure roared. 'Yet you never slept with him.'

'You're going there again?'

'But you kissed him?' He pressed on, relentless in his need to make his point.

'You can watch it on the news footage.'

He had already. Chaste, passionless kisses. She'd looked nothing like the siren who had writhed in *his* arms and pulled him closer, begging him with her body. The Princess that Damon had kissed was hot and wanton.

'The only time you kiss him is when there are cameras rolling?' He moved forward, unable to resist going nearer to her. 'You don't kiss him the way you kiss me.'

She flung her head up at that. 'Are you jealous?'

So jealous his guts burned right now. 'He doesn't want you,' he said bluntly.

Something raw flashed across her face. 'What makes you say that?'

He stopped his progress across the room and shoved his fists into his trouser pockets. 'If he wanted you the way he ought to, then he'd have moved heaven and earth to find you already. But he hasn't found you. He hasn't fought at all.'

That engagement was a political farce, so he had no reason to feel bad about cutting in and claiming what was already his. They'd sacrifice a year of their lives in sticking it out in a sham of a marriage until the baby was born. That was the only solution. Lust faded and there sure as hell was no such thing as for ever. Princess Eleni here was just going to get over her snobbishness and accept her marriage, and her divorce. And that he was no prince of a man.

* * *

Eleni inwardly flinched at that kicker. Because there it was—the cold, unvarnished truth.

Her fiancé didn't want her. Her brother found her an irritant. She had no worthwhile job. And now that her 'purity' was sullied, she'd no longer be desired as a prince's wife anyway. 'I guess my value's plummeted now I'm no longer a virgin,' she quipped sarcastically.

'Your value?' Damon's eyes blazed. 'He shouldn't give a damn about your virginity.'

His anger surprised her. 'In the way you don't?'

A different expression cut across his face. 'Oh, I care about that,' he argued in a slow, lethal whisper.

'It was none of your business,' she said haughtily.

'You don't think?' He laughed bitterly. 'That's where you're so wrong. And who you sleep with is now my business too.'

'I'm. Not. Marrying. You.' She utterly refused.

'It won't be for ever, Eleni,' he assured her dispassionately. 'We can divorce easily enough in time, without destroying the union of two entire nations,' he added pointedly. 'I will retain custody of our child. You will go back to being a princess.'

'Pardon?' The air was sucked from her lungs.

'I'll raise our child alone, without the pressure of public life.'

'What?' She stared at him, horrified to read the utterly cool seriousness on his face. 'But I'm this child's mother. A child needs her mother.' If anyone knew that, she did.

There was a thick silence.

His expression shuttered. 'A child needs parents who want her. Who love her. And if they're together, they need to be in love with each other.' His words dropped like heavy stones into a still pond. 'While we want each other, we don't—and won't—love each other. This isn't some fairy-tale romance, Eleni. This is real. And we have a real problem to deal with. As adults.'

Not a fairy tale.

She knew theirs was a connection forged by nothing but lust and hormones. But now? What he'd just said came as a greater shock than any the day had brought so far.

He wanted to take her baby from her.

'You've had a long day. You must need something to eat.' He changed the subject easily, as if he hadn't just shaken her whole foundation.

'I couldn't...' She was too shocked to contemplate something so banal as food.

'Suit yourself.' He shrugged carelessly. 'You obviously need sleep to get your head together. But starting tomorrow we'll look at ensuring your diet is appropriate.'

Appropriate? What, he thought he was going to dictate every aspect of her life now?

'How lovely of you to care,' she said acidly.

'I care about my child.' He turned his back on her. 'I'll show you to your quarters.'

Silently she followed him along the gleaming corridor of the large yacht that was still steaming full-speed away from Palisades.

He stopped almost at the end. 'You're in here,' he said briefly, gesturing through the doorway. 'I'm in the cabin next door, if you decide you do need something.'

She didn't move into the room immediately; she was too busy trying to read him. Beyond the too-handsome features, there was intense determination.

A fatalistic feeling sank into her bones. There was no escaping, no getting away from what he wanted. And he didn't actually want *her*—only her baby.

But earlier she'd felt his hardness, his heat, she'd heard his breathlessness as he'd kissed her into ecstasy. Surely he'd wanted her? But he hadn't taken her. And he could have, they both knew that.

All of which merely proved that it had been just sex for him, while she'd thought it had been somehow special…

Strain tightened his features. 'I'm not going to kiss you goodnight,' he muttered. 'I'm too tired to be able to stop it from escalating.'

As if she'd been waiting for him to kiss her? Outraged, she snarled. 'You don't think I could stop it?'

'Maybe you could,' he said doubtfully. 'But I'm not willing to take the risk.'

She stepped into the cabin and slammed the door right in his face.

Not a fairy tale.

No. This was nothing less than a nightmare. She glanced angrily at the large, smooth bed. As if she were ever going to sleep.

CHAPTER SEVEN

'ELENI.'

The whisper slipped over her skin like a warm, gentle breeze. Smiling, she snuggled deeper into the cosy cocoon.

'Eleni.'

She snapped her eyes open. Damon was leaning over her, his face only a breath from hers.

'Oh...hey... What are you doing in here?' she asked softly.

'Making sure you're okay,' he answered, equally softly.

'Why wouldn't I be?' She'd been buried deep in the best sleep she'd had in weeks.

His smile appeared—the magnetic one that had melted all her defences that night at the ball. The one she hadn't seen since. 'Well, I was wondering if you were *ever* going to wake up.'

Why would he think she wouldn't? Had he been trying to rouse her for hours already? His smile diverted her sleepy thoughts onto a different track—had he been about to try waking her with a *kiss*?

Blood quickening, she clutched the sheet to her chest and tried to sit up.

'Easy.' He held her down with a hand on her shoulder. 'Not so fast.' He sat on the edge of her bed and pointed to the bedside table. 'I brought food and water. You must be hungry now.'

The dry crackers on the plate brought her fully awake with a sharp bump. This was no fairy tale. Damon had no thought of romance, only practicality—preventing her morning sickness from surfacing.

'Thank you.' She pulled herself together, determined

to be polite and battle him with calm rationality. No more emotional outbursts that only he drew from her. All she needed now was for him to leave.

But clearly he didn't hear her unspoken plea, because he watched her expectantly. With an expressive sigh she lifted the glass of water.

'You normally sleep this late?' Damon asked.

'What time is it?'

'Almost eleven.'

She nearly spat out the mouthful of water she'd just sipped.

That amused grin flashed across his face again. 'I take it you don't usually sleep in.'

Of course not. Never in all her life.

'Has anyone been in contact?' she asked, trying to distract herself from how infuriatingly gorgeous he looked in that old tee and jeans combo.

'You're asking if they've tracked you down?' He shook his head. 'Radio silence.'

She didn't quite know how to feel about that. 'Perhaps they're planning a rescue raid and are about to break in and arrest you,' she muttered acidly. 'Any second now.'

'You came willingly.' That evil amusement lit his eyes. 'More than once.'

Uncontrollable heat washed through her, threatening an emotional outburst. Eleni levered up onto her elbow and glanced about for her robe. It wasn't there. Of course. None of her wardrobe was. The clothes she'd worn yesterday were on the floor where she'd left them. She blushed, imagining the reprimand.

Lazy, spoilt princess.

Awareness prickled. She snuck a look at him from beneath her lashes.

'Got a problem, Princess?' The slightest of jeers, low and a little rough and enough to fling her over the edge.

'Yes,' she said provocatively. 'I don't have anything fresh to wear.'

His eyes widened and for the briefest of seconds his raw reaction to her was exposed. He wanted her still. She was too thrilled by the realisation to stop.

'Hadn't thought of that in all your evil planning, had you?' she purred.

But his expression blanked. 'Maybe I felt clothes weren't going to be necessary.'

'Oh, please.'

But he'd turned that desire back on her, teasing her when she'd wanted to test him.

'You love the idea.' He leaned closer, his whispered words having that warm, magnetic effect on her most private parts. 'And as we're going to be married, there's no need to be shy.'

Her reaction to his proximity was appalling but all she wanted now was to know he was as shattered as she.

'We're *not* going to be married.' She summoned all her courage and threw back the sheet, meeting his bluff with a fierce one of her own. 'But you want me to spend the day naked?'

As he stared, she fought every instinct to curl her legs up and throw her arms around her knees. Instead she stayed still, utterly naked on the soft white linen.

His gaze travelled the length of her body—lingering on those places too private to mention. She gritted her teeth so she wouldn't squirm. But as his focus trained on her breasts, she felt the reaction—the full, tight feeling as her nipples budded and that warmth surged low within. He looked for a long, long time—and then looked lower, rendering Eleni immobile in the burning ferocity of his attention. Her skin reddened as if she'd been whipped and the slightest of goosebumps lifted. It took everything she had not to curl her toes and die of frustration.

Finally, just when she'd felt she was about to explode,

he moved. Wordlessly he pulled his tee shirt over his head and held it out to her.

Desire flooded impossibly hotter still as she stared at his bared chest. Her senses ravenously appreciated his warm tan, the ridged muscles, that light scattering of hair arrowing down to—

'Put it on,' he snapped.

She snatched it from him. But if she'd doubted whether he wanted her as much as she wanted him, she now knew.

Just sex.

She forced herself to remember that this was just sex to him. But a trickle of power flowed through her veins.

He didn't move back as she got out of the bed—he just sat there, too close, his head about level with her breasts. So she stood in front of him—refusing to be intimidated.

The tee skimmed midway down her thighs and swamped her with a sense of intimacy as his scent and warmth enveloped her. Stupidly she felt as if she were more exposed than when she'd had nothing on. Her gaze collided with his—locked, and held fast in the hot blue intensity. She wanted him to touch her again. She wanted more of that pleasure he'd pulled so easily from her last night. She was almost mad with the need for it.

'Stop looking at me like that, Princess,' he said shortly.

The rejection stung. 'Don't call me Princess.'

'Why not?' he challenged almost angrily. 'It's who you are.'

'It's not all I am,' she answered defiantly. 'I don't want that to be all I am.'

She just wanted to be Eleni. She didn't want the reminder of who she *ought* to be all the time and of her failure to do her duty.

Hormones. It had to be the hormones. Here she was facing the biggest mess of her life, rupturing the royal connection of two nations, but all she wanted was for Damon to haul her close and kiss her again. She made herself walk to the door.

'Take me back to Palisades,' she said calmly, trying to sound in control.

'So now that you've used me to hide from your brother's wrath, you want to use your brother to protect you from me.'

She turned back and saw the bitterness of Damon's smile. 'That's not—'

'No?' He shook his head in disbelief. 'Sorry, Eleni, I'm not a servant who you can order around and who'll fulfil your every whim.'

'No?' she echoed at him angrily. His opinion inflamed her. She stalked back to where he still sat braced on the edge of her bed, his fists curled into the linen. 'But that's what you said I could do. You said I could take what I wanted from you.'

'That's what you really want, isn't it?' he asked roughly, reaching out to grab her waist and hold her in front of him. 'You want me to make you feel good again.'

She wanted it so much—because she wanted it *gone*. But she knew what he wanted too. He might not like her much, but he still wanted her.

'Actually,' Eleni corrected him coolly, 'now I'm offering that to you. Take what you want from me.'

If he did that, she was sure she'd be rid of this wretched, all-encompassing desire. It was too intense—she couldn't *think* for wanting him.

His mouth tightened as he stared up at her, insolence in his expression. 'Look at Princess Sophisticated,' he jeered through gritted teeth. 'What do you think you're doing? Trying to soften me up with sex?'

She froze at the anger now darkening his eyes. 'I just don't think this needs to be that complicated.'

'This couldn't be *more* complicated. And sex only makes

things worse.' He laughed unkindly. 'I'll have you again, don't you worry about that. But only once we've reached an agreement.'

He'd laughed that night too. When she'd had the most intense experience of her life, he'd *chuckled*. Her bold pretence fell, leaving angry vulnerability in its wake.

'You can seduce me until I scream,' she said furiously. 'But you can't make me say yes to *marrying* you.'

He stood, slamming her body against his as he did.

She gasped at the intense wave of longing that flooded her. But it roused her rage with it.

'You'll never get my total surrender.' She glared up at him, even as tremors racked her traitorous body as he pressed her against his rock-hard heat.

'And I don't want it,' he growled back, rolling his hips against hers in a demonstration of pure, sensual power. 'Lust passes.'

She hoped to heaven he was right. But his smug superiority galled her. 'You just have to know it all, don't you?'

But she didn't need another overprotective male trying to control every aspect of her life.

His gaze narrowed. 'I only want what's best for my baby.' He released her and stalked to the door, turning to hit her with his parting shot. 'We will marry. The baby will be born legitimately. And ultimately my child will live a safe, free life. With me.'

He slammed the door, leaving her recoiling at his cold-hearted plan. Shame slithered at her lame attempt to seduce him, suffocating the remnants of the heat he'd stirred too easily. He was too strong, too clinical when she'd been confused with desire. She was such a fool.

But that he truly planned to take her child horrified her. She had to fight him on that. She had to win.

Eleni snatched up her skirt. She marched out to the lounge to confront Damon again, only to catch sight of the large screen revealed on the wall. The sound was muted, but she recognised the image. Stunned, she stepped forward to look more closely.

Bunches and bunches of flowers and cards from well-wishers were placed at the gates of Palisades palace. The camera zoomed in on one of the bunches and she read the 'get well soon' message written—to *her*. Giorgos had taken her idea literally and told the world she was too unwell to embark on her tour with Prince Xander.

'There are so many.' She sank onto the nearest sofa.

'Why are you so surprised?' Damon walked forward and sat in the chair at an angle to her sofa, his voice cool. 'You're their perfect Princess.'

She rubbed her forehead. She was an absolute fraud and all those people were being kind when she didn't deserve it.

'It's not a total lie. You *don't* feel well,' he added gruffly.

'I've made a mess of everything.'

'So marry me. We'll live together away from Palisades until the baby is born.'

And then he was going to take her child from her.

Suddenly she broke; tears stung her eyes even as she laughed hopelessly. 'The stupid thing is, I don't even know for sure that I am pregnant.'

'Pardon?'

Of course she was pregnant. She knew it. She was late and there were all those other signs—morning sickness, tender breasts...

'Eleni?' Damon prompted sharply.

She sighed. 'I haven't done a test.'

He gazed at her, astounded. 'How can you not have done a test?'

'How could I?' She exploded, leaping back to her feet because she couldn't contain her frustration a second longer. 'How would I get a test without everyone finding out?' She paced, railing at the confines of the luxurious room and of the life she was bound by. 'I don't even do my own personal shopping—how can I when I don't even carry my own damn *money*?' She'd never shopped alone in all her life. She registered the dumbfounded amazement on Damon's face.

'I don't have any income,' she explained furiously. 'If I want anything I just ask someone and it arrives. Is that someone now you?' She gestured wildly at him. 'I don't have a money card, Damon. Or any cash. I've never needed it. I know that makes me spoilt. But it also makes me helpless.' It was beyond humiliating to be so dependent. 'It makes me useless.'

She flopped back down on the sofa and buried her face in her hands, mortified at the sting of fresh tears. So much for controlling her emotional outbursts.

'All this effort you've gone to, to steal me away might be based on one massive mistake.' She laughed bitterly at the irony. Wouldn't that just serve him right?

Damon hunched down in front of her, his hands on her knees. 'Eleni.'

His voice was too soft. Too calm.

'What?' She peered at him.

He studied her, his expression uncharacteristically solemn. 'Even if you're not pregnant, could you really marry him now?'

'Because I've spent the night on board a boat with another man and no chaperone?' She glared at him, hating that old-school reasoning and the expectation that she'd stay 'pure'—when no prince, no man, ever had to.

But Damon shook his head. 'Because you don't love him. You don't even want him.' He cocked his head, a vestige of that charming smile tweaking his lips. 'At least you want me.'

She closed her eyes. She *hated* him. And she hated how much she wanted him.

There was nothing but silence from Damon. She realised he'd left the room but a moment later he returned, a small rectangular box in his hand.

'You always have pregnancy tests on board?' Humiliation washed over her at her ineptitude.

'No. But as I suspected you were pregnant, I thought it might be useful.' So easily he'd done what she was unable to.

She snatched the box from his outstretched hand. 'I'll be back in a minute.'

CHAPTER EIGHT

DAMON GAZED DOWN at the distressed woman who'd word-lessly waved a small plastic stick at him as she returned to his sofa. The positive proof hit him—she truly had no clue. Her one escape plan had simply been to *hide* and now she was lost. Her lies yesterday had been those of an inexpe-rienced, overly sheltered girl trying to brazen her way out of a dire situation.

He grimaced—was he actually feeling sorry for her now? Fool.

She could be confident when she wanted and had strength when she needed it. She was *spoilt*, that was her problem. Utterly used to getting her own way and never having to wait. He gritted his teeth as he remembered the way she'd flung back her bed coverings and taunted him. So brazen. So innocent. So damned gorgeous he was still struggling to catch his breath.

But she was going to have to wait for that now. And so was he.

Never had he understood how his father could have com-pletely betrayed his mother. Why he'd risked everything he'd worked so hard to achieve. But now Damon understood all too well what could cloud a man's reason and make him forget his responsibilities and priorities.

Shameless lust. The age-old tale of desire.

He was not making the mistakes of his father. He was not abandoning his child to illegitimacy. But nor would he remain in a loveless marriage for years on end.

'You need to marry me, to protect the baby.' He tried to stay calm, but her repeated refusals were galling.

He'd never allow his child to be used for political manoeuvring. His baby would be raised in a safe environment with him. Their divorce would be better than being trapped in a home where the parents tolerated each other only for 'the look of it'.

Eleni paled.

'You know that, away from the palace, my child can have a normal life.' He tried to speak reasonably. 'Not hounded by press or burdened by duty.'

He saw her mouth tremble. He'd known this was how he'd get to her. She'd told him earlier—she didn't want to be *only* a princess.

'*I* can give this child everything,' she argued.

'Really? Can you give her complete freedom? With me, she can be free to do whatever she wants. Study whatever, live wherever. No pressure to perform.'

'And your life isn't in the public eye?' she queried sharply. 'Don't you billionaires get picked for "most eligible" lists in magazines?'

'When you're not a prince and therefore not public property, privacy can be paid for.'

'But this child will be a prince—or princess,' she pointed out, her voice roughening. 'And you can't deny this child his or her birthright.'

'The child can decide whether to take on a royal role when it's old enough.'

Eleni laughed at him. 'You think it's something you can just *choose*?'

'Why not?' Damon challenged her.

She shook her head. 'Giorgos would never allow it.'

'I don't give a damn what Giorgos wants.'

'But I do. Since our father died, he's been brother, father and mother to me and all the while he has that huge job. The hours he works—you have no idea…' She trailed off, pain shadowing her eyes.

Damon remembered when the King had died just over a

decade ago. His father had returned to Palisades for the funeral and taken an extra week to visit his long-term lover—Kassie's mother. Grimly Damon shoved that bitter memory aside. But he couldn't recall much about the Queen at all. He frowned at Eleni. 'Where's your mother?'

Eleni looked shocked. Then she drew in a deep breath. 'She died twenty minutes after giving birth to me.' Despite that steadying breath, her voice shook. 'So I know what it's like not to have a mother. And I know what it's like to have your parent too busy to be around to listen... I want to be there for my child. And I will be. In all the ways she or he needs. *Always.*'

Damon stared at her fixedly, ignoring her passion and focusing on the salient information. Her mother had died in childbirth.

He pulled out his phone. 'You need to see a doctor.'

Eleni gaped at him, then visibly collected herself. 'I'm not sure if you know how this works, Damon, but the baby isn't due for *months*.'

So what? She needed the best care possible from this moment on.

'Just because my mother died in childbirth, doesn't mean that I might have trouble,' she added stiffly.

'You need a basic check-up at the very least.'

'Because you don't trust me to take care of myself?'

Blood pounding in his ears, he ignored her petulance. Quickly he scrolled through his contacts to find his physician and tapped out a text asking him to find the best obstetrician he knew. Sure, women gave birth round the world almost every minute, but not always in full health and Eleni's news had caught him by surprise.

'I don't need cotton-wool treatment.' Her tone sharpened.

'I don't intend to give it to you,' he muttered, feeling better for having started the search. 'But I'm not going to ignore your condition either.'

'It's just pregnancy, not an *illness*,' she rasped. 'And I am sensible enough to ensure I get the best treatment when I get back to shore. Trust me, I don't want to die. But you can't make me see someone I don't want to see, nor stop me from doing the things I like.'

Looking at her was always a mistake—especially when she was passionate and vitality flowed from her glowing skin. Had people stopped her doing the things she'd liked in the past? He couldn't resist a tease. 'And what do you like?'

She glared at him, picking up the heavy innuendo he'd intended. 'Not that.'

He laughed even as a wave of protectiveness surged. 'Did you know some women have a heightened libido when pregnant?'

'I'm not one of those women.'

Her prim reply was undermined by the quickening of her breath. It spurred him to tease her more. 'No, you have the appetite of a nymphomaniac all the time.'

'I do not.'

'Yeah, you do.' He laughed again at her outraged expression. But that sensual blush had spread over her skin and sparks lit up her green-blue eyes.

There was no denying the chemistry between them. But he'd not realised just how inexperienced she was in all areas of life—not just the bedroom. Not to have access to cash? To have any normal kind of freedom?

Yes, she was spoilt, but she was unspoilt in other ways. She'd been too sheltered for her own good. And finally he could understand why. She was the precious baby who'd lost her mother far too soon. Raised by her bereft, too-busy father, and then a brother too young and too burdened to know how to care for a young girl and let her grow. All they'd wanted to do was protect her.

It was a sentiment Damon was starting to understand too well.

And now guilt crept in. He regretted the horrible scenario he'd painted—threatening to take her child from her. What kind of cold-hearted jerk was he?

But he'd been angered by her constant refusals and he'd lashed out, instinctively striking where it would hurt most. He drew in a calming breath. He'd win her acceptance with care, not cruelty.

'So it was the three of you, until your father died?' he asked, wanting to understand her background more.

'My father was a very busy man,' Eleni answered softly. 'He was the King—he had a lot to occupy his time. So for a long while it was Giorgos and me. He's a bit older, but he was always fun.' Her expression warmed briefly. 'When Father died, Giorgos took over.'

'Giorgos was young for that.'

'He is very highly regarded,' she said loyally.

'You're close.'

Her gaze slid from his. 'He has a big job to do. Back then he knew some of the courtiers didn't think he was old enough to handle the responsibility—'

'So he worked twice as hard to prove them wrong.' Damon smiled at her surprised look. 'It's understandable.'

She gazed out of the window. 'He's not stopped working since.'

And she was left lonely in her little turret in the palace. Damon saw how easily it had happened. She was loyal and sweet but also trapped and stifled.

'I'm supposed to marry a royal,' she said quietly. 'It's tradition. I know you think it's stupid, but it's how it's always been. I wanted to do the right thing for Giorgos.'

'Well, I'm not a prince and I never will be.' Damon took a seat. 'But won't it be easier to divorce me, a commoner, than cause conflict with two countries if you divorce your Prince?'

Her lips tightened. 'I'm not supposed to get divorced,' she said quietly. 'That's not part of the fairy tale.'

'Times change. Even royals live in the real world, Eleni. And they get divorced.'

She looked anywhere but at him. 'I barely know you.'

'Do you know Prince Xander?' Damon asked bluntly.

The shake of her head was almost imperceptible.

'Then what's the difference between marrying him and marrying me?' His muscles pulled tighter and tighter still in the face of her silence. The urge to go to her, to kiss her into acquiescence, made him ache. Despite her denial earlier he knew he could do it. All he'd have to do was kiss her and she'd be breathless and begging and he needed to get away from her before he did exactly that. He wanted to hear her say yes to him without that. 'Am I an ogre?'

'You want to take my child from me.'

'And you tried to deny the child was mine. I figure that makes us even.' He stood, unable to remain in the same room as her without succumbing to reckless action. 'Take your time to think about your options, Eleni. I'm in no rush to go anywhere.'

Why didn't she want to marry Damon? Eleni couldn't answer that honestly—not to him when she could barely admit the truth to herself. She'd never wanted anyone the way she wanted him. Her marriage to Xander would have been a loveless union. But safe compared to the tempestuous gamut of emotions Damon roused in her. She was terrified of what might happen to her heart if she stayed with him for long.

She scoffed at her inner dramatics. She needed to grow up and get a grip on her sexual frustration. Because that was all this was, right? Her first case of raw lust.

She turned off the large computer screen and foraged in the bookcase lining one of the walls, her thoughts circling around and around until her stomach rumbled and she realised how ravenous she was.

Quietly she left the room and found her way to a sleek

galley kitchen. No one was in there, thank goodness, because she was starving. She located the pantry, pouncing on an open box of cereal.

'You okay?'

'Oh.' She swallowed hastily as she turned. 'You caught me.'

He had been swimming, probably in the pool on deck. Eleni stared, fascinated by the droplets of water slowly snaking down his bronzed chest until they were finally caught in the towel he'd slung low around his hips.

'Not yet.' He walked forward. 'What are you doing that is so awful?'

Staring at your bare chest.

'I shouldn't have helped myself,' she mumbled. 'Eating straight from the packet.'

'That's not awful. That's survival instinct.' He reached into the box she was holding and helped himself to a couple of the cereal clusters. 'Don't you go into the kitchen at the palace?'

She shook her head, forcing herself to swallow.

'You just ask one of the servants?'

'What do you expect?' She bristled. 'I live in a palace and that comes with privileges.'

'But what if you wanted to just make a sandwich?'

'Then someone makes it for me.'

'You never wanted to make your own sandwich?'

'It's not my place to.' She refused to rise to his baiting. 'I'm not going to take someone's job from them.'

He looked at her as she snaffled another cereal snack. 'What would you have done if being a princess wasn't your place?'

'I studied languages and art history.' She shrugged. 'I'd probably teach.'

'But what would you have done if you could have chosen anything?'

Eleni sighed. 'My brother loves me very much but he is

very busy and most of my education was left to an older advisor who had ancient ideas about the role of a princess.'

'You're there to be decorative.'

'And quiet and serene—'

'Serene?' He laughed. 'You're a screamer.'

She sent him a filthy look.

'So?' He teased, but pressed the point. 'What would you have done?'

'I wanted to be a vet.' But she'd known it was impossible. The hours of study too intense when she had public duties to perform as well.

'A vet?' He looked taken aback.

'I like dogs.' She shrugged.

'You have dogs?'

'I had a gorgeous spaniel when I was younger.'

'So why not vet school? Did you not have the grades?'

'Of course I had the grades.' She gritted her teeth and turned away because she knew where he was going with this, so she didn't tell him she'd wanted to do Fine Arts first. Again she'd been denied—too frivolous. She was a princess and she had to remain demure and humble. But was hers really such an awful life to bestow upon a child? Yes, there were restrictions, but there was also such privilege. Couldn't she make it different?

'You know I can offer our child a level of freedom that you can't,' Damon said. 'Isn't that what you want, your child not to have to "perform" the way you've had to all your life?'

'I want the best for my child in every way,' Eleni said calmly. And she knew exactly what she had to do for her child now. Nothing was ever going to be the same. She sucked in one last deep breath. 'They're all going to figure out that I was pregnant when we married.'

He stilled; his gaze glittered. 'Either we lie and say the baby was born prematurely, or we say nothing at all.' He cleared his throat. 'The second option gets my vote.

There will always be whispers and Internet conspiracy theories but we rise above it with a dignified silence and carry on.'

She nodded. 'I understand what you're saying about giving our child freedom, but I'm its mother and I won't walk away from it. Ever.' She braced and pushed forward. 'If you're serious about doing what's best for our child, then you won't ask me to.'

He carefully leaned against the bench. 'So you'll marry me.'

'If we work out a plan. For after.' When their marriage ended, it needed to be smooth. 'I think there are precedents in other countries for a child not to take a royal title,' she said bravely. Giorgos would have a fit but she would have to try to make him understand. 'We can keep him or her out of the limelight and work out some kind of shared custody arrangement.'

Her heart tore at the thought, but her child had the right to be loved by both its parents.

'Then we'll work it out.' Damon looked out of the window.

'So now you've got what you wanted,' Eleni said.

He looked back at her. His blue eyes had darkened almost to black. 'And what's that?'

'Me. Saying yes.' She watched, surprised to see his tension was even more visible than before. 'What, you're not satisfied?'

'No.'

'Then what do you want?'

He took the two steps to bring himself smack bang in front of her. 'I want my tee shirt back.'

Desire uncoiled low and strong in her belly. 'But I'm not wearing anything underneath it.'

'Good.' His blunt expression of want felled her.

'Are you wearing anything under the skirt?' he asked roughly, gripping the hem of the tee.

She could barely shake her head. 'I thought you said this would only complicate things.'

'Now we're in agreement on the big issues, we can handle a little complication.'

He tugged the tee shirt up. She lifted her arms and in a second it was gone. She was bared to his gaze, his touch, his tongue.

She gasped as he swooped. There was no denying this. He desired her body. Fine. She desired his. Reason dissolved under sensual persuasion. He pressed the small of her back—holding her still, keeping her close, until he growled something unintelligible and picked her up to sit her on the edge of the bench. He pushed her knees apart so he could stand between them. Elation soared through Eleni.

This was what she wanted.

His kiss was nothing less than ravaging. She moaned as he plundered, his tongue seeking, tasting, taking everything and she did more than let him. She gave—straining closer. She wound her arms around his neck, arching and aching. His hands swept down her body, igniting sensation, sparking that deeper yearning. He slid his warm palm under her skirt. She trembled as he neared where she was wet and ready. His kiss became more rapacious still as he touched her so intimately, and her moan melted in his mouth. He lifted away only to tease her more—kissing the column of her neck, down to her collarbones and then to the aching, full breasts pointing hard for his attention.

But the nagging feeling inside wouldn't ease—resistance to this hedonism. It had been wrong before; it was still wrong now. She closed her eyes, turning her face to the side as heat blistered her from the inside out.

'Don't hide.' He nudged her chin. 'Let me see you.'

'I can't,' she muttered, desperately turning her face away.

He pulled back completely, forcing her to look into his eyes. 'You're not cheating. Your engagement is broken now.'

She was ashamed that he knew her desire for him had

overruled her duty and her loyalty. Her engagement to Xander had been a loveless arrangement, but Damon was right. She was an appalling person.

'This is nothing much more than what happened yesterday.' Damon tempted her again.

Wrong. It was so much more. If she let him in again, she wasn't sure she could cope. The passion was all-consuming, addictive and all she could think about at a time when she should be concerned with her family. With her duty. But she couldn't think clearly when she was within five hundred paces of this man.

And she doubted him. He'd wanted to find her after the ball only because he'd known there was a risk of pregnancy, not because he'd wanted more time with her. He was only taking advantage of the situation now—certainly it wasn't that he liked her.

But he'd *wanted* her when he *hadn't* known who she was. He wasn't going for the 'perfect Princess' that night, he'd wanted just *her*. There was something still seductive about that.

Damon was studying her too intently. It was as if he could strip back all her defences and see into her poor, inexperienced soul.

'Why didn't you tell me you were a virgin?' he asked softly.

There was no point holding back the truth now. 'Because you would have stopped.'

He expelled a harsh breath and framed her face with surprisingly gentle hands. 'You could have said you were inexperienced.'

'I was pretending I wasn't,' she muttered, mortified. The mask, the costume had combined to make her feel confident. He'd made her feel sexy and invincible. Unstoppable. 'I had a persona that night...now I don't.'

'Are you sure it was a persona?' Damon challenged. 'Or

was it the true you?' He skimmed the tips of his fingers down her neck until she shivered.

Was she that person? That woman who took such risks—and found such pleasure?

You want more than what you think you should have.

'There is nothing wrong with liking this, Eleni.' He tempted her to the point of madness.

'But I like it too much.' She confessed that last secret on the merest thread of a breath. 'It's not *me*. It scares me.'

That was why she'd resisted his proposal initially. The intensity of her desire for him terrified her.

His expression tightened. 'I scare you?'

'Not you. Me,' she muttered. 'I never behave like this. Like *that*.' She was appalled at how she'd behaved that night and since. All those outbursts? The waves of emotion? 'You were right. I lied. I cheated. I'm every bit that awful, spoilt person you said I was.'

Damon shifted away from her.

Eleni watched, suddenly chilled at the loss of contact. Her body yearned for the closeness of his again. But he'd switched it off. How could he do that so easily?

Hurt and alarm hit. She shouldn't have spoken so rashly. She shouldn't have stopped him because at least she could've been rid of the frustration that now cut deeper than ever.

'You need to be at peace before this happens again,' Damon said quietly—too damn in control. 'Then you won't need to hide. Then you can truly let go.'

She watched, amazed and horrified as he walked to the doorway. How, exactly, was she supposed to find peace when he was making the decision for her? When he was leaving her this...*needy*.

'I hate you,' she called. One last emotional outburst.

'I'm sure.' Damon glanced back with a smile. 'I'd never dream that you could love me.'

CHAPTER NINE

'I'M NOT WAITING for Giorgos to hunt me down like some fugitive. I want to go to him.' Eleni braced for Damon's response as she sat opposite him at the table the next morning.

She wasn't letting him make all the decisions any more. After the most desultory dinner, she'd spent the night mentally practising her confrontations with both Damon and Giorgos and it was time to put both plans into reality.

Damon arched a sardonic eyebrow. 'Good morning, fire-breathing warrior woman, who are you and what have you done with my meek fiancée?'

'I need to see him,' she insisted.

Damon's answering smile was uncomfortably wicked. 'The yacht turned around last night. We'll be back at Palisades in less than an hour. I've just let him know I have you.'

Eleni stared as his words knocked the wind from her sails.

'Well.' It was going to happen so much sooner than she'd expected. She puffed out a deep breath but it didn't settle her speeding heart. 'We might want to let him know I'm safe on board, otherwise he might try to blow up your boat.'

Damon chuckled. 'I thought Palisades was a peace-loving nation.'

It was, but when Damon's yacht entered the marina, Eleni's nerves tightened unbearably. Never before had she defied Giorgos's wishes and now the weight of his inevitable disappointment was crushing.

'I should handle him by myself,' she said to Damon

as she counted the number of soldiers waiting on the pier ready to escort her. It was a heavy-handed display of her brother's authority. 'I should have done that in the first place.'

Damon turned his back on the waiting men with an arrogant lift to his chin. Apparently he was unfazed by the latent aggression waiting for them. 'I'll stay silent if that's what you wish, but I will be beside you.'

Because he didn't trust her?

Except there was something in Damon's eyes. Something more than protectiveness and more than possessiveness. She turned away, not trusting her own vision. Because the last thing she deserved was tenderness.

The military men wordlessly ushered them into a car and drove them straight to the palace. The gleaming building felt silent, as if everyone were collectively holding their breath—waiting for Giorgos's explosion. For the first time in her life Eleni felt like a stranger in her own home. The only person not tiptoeing on eggshells was Damon. He casually strolled the endless corridors as if he hadn't a care in the world.

They weren't taken to either her private suite or to Giorgos's. Instead her brother's assistant led them to a formal room usually reserved for meetings with visiting Heads of State. Chilled, Eleni paused in the doorway. Giorgos grimly waited in full King mode—white dress uniform, jacket laden with medals and insignia, boots polished to mirror-like sheen. All that was missing was his crown.

'I've cancelled an engagement at the last minute. Again.' Giorgos fixed a steely stare on Damon.

But her brother's barely disguised loathing apparently bounced off as Damon blandly stared right back.

'You took advantage of an innocent,' Giorgos accused shortly. 'You seduced her.'

Was she invisible? Straightening her shoulders, Eleni stepped forward.

'Maybe I seduced him.' She clenched her fists to hide how badly her hands were shaking, but she was determined to take control of this conversation. *She* was having the input here, not Damon.

Her brother finally bothered to look at her, but as he faced her he became like a marble sculpture. Expressionless and unreadable.

'Damon and I will be married as soon as possible,' she said, determined to state her case before he tore her to shreds.

Giorgos continued to look unmoved. 'Last time we spoke you insisted you were not marrying either Prince Xander or Mr Gale.'

'I was upset,' she conceded coolly. 'But this is the best course of action, Giorgos.'

'He is not a prince. He has no title whatsoever.'

Of course her brother knew Damon's background already—he'd have had his investigators on it from the moment he'd gotten the message this morning. From Giorgos's frown, Damon's success mattered little to him. 'You know the expectations—'

'Change the law, create a new custom.' For the second time in her life Eleni dared to interrupt her brother. 'You're King. You have the power.'

'And should I abuse power trusted to me, for personal gain?'

'Is it personal gain, or would you simply be granting the same right that any other citizen in Palisades already has?' Why couldn't she have the right to choose for herself?

Giorgos's eyes narrowed. 'So I simply ignore centuries of custom and duty? I abandon all levels of diplomacy and the expectations of our important neighbours and alliances?'

'My personal life shouldn't be used for political manoeuvring.'

'So you got yourself pregnant instead of simply making that argument?'

She recoiled in shock and her anger unleashed. 'Of course I didn't. But would you be listening to me if I *wasn't* pregnant?'

Giorgos sent Damon the iciest look she'd ever seen. 'You know about our mother?'

'Yes. I will ensure Eleni receives care from the best specialists.'

Giorgos shook his head. 'Our doctor is ready to give her a check-up now.'

Eleni gaped. Did her brother think she was somehow incapacitated?

Damon answered before she could. 'I don't think that's necessary—'

'It is entirely necessary. She must be—'

'Stop trying to overrule each other.' Eleni interrupted Giorgos again, her heart and head pounding. 'My medical decisions will be made by *me*.'

'Dr Vecolli is already here,' Giorgos insisted.

'I'm not seeing Dr Vecolli.'

'He's been our family physician for twenty years.'

'Which is exactly *why* I'm not seeing him. He's like a grandfather to me. I would like to see a female doctor.' She glared as Giorgos frowned at her. 'What, do you think no woman can be a doctor, or is it just me you thought so incapable I couldn't even be trusted with animals?'

'I once wanted to be an airplane pilot.' Giorgos dripped cold sarcasm. 'But you *know* we cannot hold down a full-time job while fulfilling royal duty. It is impossible.'

'Why?' she challenged. 'Couldn't I be useful other than cutting ribbons and awarding prizes?'

'You're going to have your hands full with your baby, or had you forgotten that?'

Eleni flared anew at Giorgos's patronising tone. 'So while plenty of other mothers work, I can only be a brood mare? Do you think I'm that incompetent?' She was out-raged—and *hurt*.

'I don't think you're—' Her brother broke off and ran a hand through his hair.

'Why are we so enslaved by the past?' she asked him emotionally. 'Just because things have always been done a certain way, doesn't mean they always have to continue in that same way.' And she was more capable than he believed her to be—wasn't she?

Giorgos was silent for a long moment. Then he sighed softly. 'Then how do you plan to manage this?'

'By marrying Damon. I'll have the baby and then...' She drew in a steadying breath. 'Beyond that, I don't really know. But I don't want all those limitations on me any more. They're untenable.'

She braced for his response. She couldn't yet tell him her marriage had an end date already. One let-down at a time was enough.

Giorgos's expression revealed more now. But he didn't need to worry; this wedding wouldn't end the world.

'It could be leaked that Eleni was corralled into the wedding with Prince Xander.' Damon broke the tense silence. 'She was too afraid to stand up to you and the Prince. Public sympathy will be on her side if it is cast as a forbidden love story.'

She didn't deserve public sympathy.

'She fell in love with me during her secret hospital visits.' Damon embroidered the possible story. 'But you refused your consent for her to have a relationship with a commoner. She was so distraught she really did get sick. Only then did you realise how serious she was.'

Eleni winced at the scenario he'd painted. Did everyone need to know she'd been unable to stand up for herself? More importantly, it didn't do her brother justice.

'Do we need to make Giorgos sound such a bully?' She frowned.

Giorgos's eyes widened with an arrested expression.

'Prince Xander is still the injured party,' Damon continued after a beat. 'But it can be spun that they'd not spent much time together. Therefore her defection won't make him appear any less attractive.'

Eleni smothered her startled laugh. Damon was light years more attractive than Xander.

For a long moment Giorgos studied the painting hanging on the wall opposite him. With every passing second Eleni's heart sank—recriminations and rejection were inevitable.

'You might have met your match, Eleni.' Giorgos slowly turned to her, the wryest of smiles in his eyes. 'He won't curl round your little finger.'

'The way you do?' Eleni dared to breathe back.

'You will be married in the private chapel today.' Giorgos's steely seriousness returned. 'I will release a public proclamation together with a few photographs. You will not make a public appearance. Rather you will go away for at least a month.'

'Away?' Eleni was stunned at the speed of his agreement.

'You need to get your personal situation stable while this fluff is spread in the press.' Giorgos's sarcasm edged back. 'You'll go to France. I have a safe house there.'

'But the safest house of all is this one,' Eleni argued. She was not letting her brother banish her. Not when she had to get to grips with a husband she barely knew and to whom she could hardly control her reaction. Staying home would give her the space and privacy to deal with Damon.

'Remaining in Palisades would give Damon a chance to learn palace protocol and understand the expectations for our...*future*.' She glanced at Damon, fudging just how short their future together was going to be.

Damon shrugged but his eyes were sharp. 'I'm happy to hang here for a while if that's what you wish, Eleni.'

'I am scheduled to spend a few weeks at the Sum-

mer House,' Giorgos said stiffly. 'So that would work.'
He turned icily to Damon. 'But understand that I will be
watching you, even from there. I don't trust you.'

'Fair enough,' Damon answered equally coolly. 'If I
were you, I wouldn't either.' He smiled as if he hadn't a
care in the world. 'I'll not take a title, by the way. I'll remain Damon Gale.'

'While I'll remain Princess Eleni Nicolaides,' Eleni answered instantly.

'And the child will be Prince or Princess Nicolaides-
Gale—we get it,' Giorgos snapped. 'Let's just get everything formalised and documented before it leaks. I expect
you at the chapel in an hour. Both of you looking the part.'

Her brother stalked towards the door, his posture ema-
nating *uptight King*.

'I'll send someone to the yacht to fetch a suit,' Damon
drawled once Giorgos had left. 'I guess you'd better go
magic up a wedding dress.'

She stared at her fiancé and clapped a hand over her
mouth in horror.

'Don't worry.' Damon's satisfied smile turned distinctly
wicked. 'You can wear as little as you like—I will not say
no. That busty blue number you wore at the ball would be
nice—'

Flushing hotly, Eleni swiftly walked out on him, desperately needing a moment alone to process everything.
But her maid hovered at the door to her suite, the woman's
expression alert with unmistakable excitement.

'Oh, Bettina. I'm sorry I've been away.' Eleni quickly
pasted on a smile. 'And I'm not back for long.'

Bettina nodded eagerly. 'I have done the best I can in
the last half hour. I've hung the samples so you can choose.
There are nine altogether—from New York, Paris, and one
from Milan.'

'Samples?' Eleni repeated, confused.

'The wedding dresses.'

Nine wedding dresses? Eleni gaped. If that wasn't being spoilt, she didn't know what was.

'Would you like to try them on?'

Eleni saw the sparkle in her maid's eyes and realised the fiction that Eleni was marrying her long-secret love had already spread. She drew in a deep breath and made her smile bigger. 'Absolutely.'

But her smile became a wide 'oh' as Bettina wheeled out the garment rack she'd hung the gowns on. And then Eleni surrendered to vain delight—at the very least she could look good on her wedding day.

The sixth option was the winner; she knew as soon as she stepped into it. It was exactly what she'd choose for *herself*—not as something befitting 'Princess Eleni'. The sleek dress with its svelte lines and delicate embroidery was subtle but sexy and she loved it.

As Eleni walked away from her maid, her suite and her life as she knew it, butterflies skittered around her stomach, but she determinedly kept her smile on her face.

She couldn't let the fairy-tale image fall apart just yet.

Giorgos stood waiting for her at the entrance to the private chapel. Her smile—and her footsteps—faltered as she saw his frown deepening. But this might be her only chance to speak to him privately.

'I'm sorry I let you down,' she said when she was close enough for only him to hear.

'You haven't.' Her brother held out a small posy of roses for her.

Tears sprang to her eyes as she took the pretty bouquet from him. 'Thank you,' she whispered.

He nodded, stiffly. 'Do you love him?' Giorgos suddenly asked.

The direct question stole her breath. For the first time that she could recall, her brother looked awkward—almost unsure—as he gazed hard at a spot on the floor just ahead of them.

She couldn't be anything but honest. 'I don't know.'

That frown furrowed his brow again. 'Make it work, Eleni.'

Then he held out his arm, that glimpse of uncertainty gone. She nodded, unable to speak given the lump in her throat, and placed her hand in the crook of his elbow.

As Giorgos escorted her into the chapel, Eleni caught sight of Damon standing at the altar. He was dressed in a stunningly tailored suit. He seemed taller, broader; his eyes were very blue. He claimed the attention of every one of her senses. Every thought. Her pulse raced, her limbs trembled. She tried to remember to breathe. She couldn't possibly be *excited*, could she? This was only part of the plan to secure her child's legitimacy and freedom. This was only for her baby.

But those butterflies danced a complicated reel.

It's just a contract. It's only for the next year. It doesn't mean anything...

But reciting her vows to Damon in the family chapel heightened her sense of reverence. Here—in front of her brother, in front of him, in this sanctuary and symbol of all things past and future—she had to promise to love him.

He's the father of my child.

She could love him only for that, couldn't she? It wasn't a lie.

But a whisper of foreboding swept down her spine and she shivered just as Damon turned towards her. She met his gaze, almost frozen by the enormity of their actions.

But Damon wasn't frozen. He had that slightly wicked expression in his eyes as he reached to pull her close.

The kiss sealing their wedding contract should have been businesslike, but he lingered a fraction too long. That heat coursed through her veins. She closed her eyes and in that instant was lost. Her bones ached and the instinct to lean into him overwhelmed her. Only at the exact moment of her surrender, he suddenly pulled away. She caught a glimpse of wildness in his eyes but then her lifetime of training took over. She turned and walked with him out of the chapel and into the formal throne room. There she dutifully posed for endless photos with Giorgos on one side of her, Damon on the other. She smiled and smiled and smiled. Perfectly Princess Eleni.

Her brother took her hand and bowed. 'You make a beautiful bride, Eleni.'

Because all that mattered was how she looked and how this arrangement looked to the world? But Giorgos's expression softened and he suddenly gave her a quick hug.

'Take care of yourself.' With the briefest of glances at Damon, her brother left.

A little dazed, Eleni gazed after him. It had been years since he'd hugged her. Her nerves lightened. The worst was over, right? Now she could move forward.

'Eleni.'

She turned.

Damon stood too close, too handsome, his expression too knowing. That little respite from inner tension was over as she realised the first night of her marriage lay ahead. The beginning of the end of the thing neither of them had wanted in the first place.

'We should take a couple of photos somewhere less formal,' Damon suggested.

Eleni shook her head as his glance around the ornate room revealed his less than impressed opinion.

'There's nowhere "less formal" anywhere in this palace,' she informed him with perverse pleasure.

'What about outside?' Damon eyed up the French doors that no one had opened in Eleni's life.

'That's locked,' she said.

Damon turned the handle and the door opened silently and easily on the hinge.

Of course it did.

He sent her a triumphant smile that did even more annoying things to her insides.

'You're the most irritating creature alive,' she grumbled.

'I know,' he commiserated drolly. 'But you still want me.'

'What are you doing?' she whispered, stalking outside to get away from him as much as anything.

'This is your palace, Eleni. You're allowed to run around in it, right?' He was still too close.

'You're…'

'What?' he challenged, arrogance in his eyes as he wrapped his arm around her waist, stopping her flight and drawing her close. 'What am I?'

Not good for her health.

Eleni half laughed, half groaned as she gave into temptation and leaned against him. But she refused to answer.

Damon retaliated physically. Magically. Reigniting those embers settled so slightly beneath her skin. The kiss banished the last butterflies and a bonfire burned, engulfing her body in a delicious torture of desire. This time he held nothing back, pulling her close enough for her to feel just how she affected him. Desire flared, compounded by the awareness that, this time, there was nothing to stop them.

Click. Click, click, click.

She put her hands on his broad chest and pushed, remembering too late there was a freaking photographer following them.

'I'm the Princess,' she muttered, mainly to remind herself.

But Damon kept her close with one arm around her waist and a light grip on her jaw. 'I didn't marry "the Princess".'

'Yes, you did.' There was no separating who she was

from what she was. She had to accept that and now he did too.

The photographer looked disappointed when Damon sent him away. As he left, thudding blades whirred overhead and she glanced up to see her brother's helicopter swiftly heading north.

'So now we're alone,' Damon said softly. 'And not a second too soon.'

She suppressed the shiver at the determination in his tone and gazed at the rings on her finger to avoid looking at him. He'd surprised her in the chapel, sliding an engagement ring on her finger as well as a wedding band.

'You don't like them?' he asked, inexorably escorting her towards that open French door.

On the contrary, she loved them, but she was wary of showing it. She couldn't quite make out his mood. Was he angry as well as aroused? 'How did you pick them so quickly?'

A grim smile briefly curved his mouth. 'I had just a little longer to prepare for our wedding than you did.'

Even so, his organisational skills were impressive. 'It's a sapphire?'

He shook his head. 'A blue diamond for my blue bride.'

Her heart knocked. The stone's colour was the exact shade of the dress she'd worn that fateful night.

'You still look blue.' He cocked his head curiously. 'Why? You have the support of your brother. Everything that mattered has been resolved. So why so sad?'

Because this wasn't going to last. Because for all the foolishness in the garden, this was as much of a charade as her wedding to Xander would have been. Because she was a romantic fool. Part of her had wanted real love on her wedding day.

You can't be a child any more, Eleni. You're having a child.

Unable to answer his demanding tone, she walked

through the palace towards her private apartment. There wasn't a servant or soldier to be seen, as if by some silent decree they knew to stay out of sight. And it was a good thing too. She'd seen the banked heat in Damon's eyes. She knew he wasn't about to show her any mercy.

Her pulse skittered, speeding up the nearer she got to her rooms. At the foot of the staircase he reached out and took her hand.

She tried to hide the quickening of her breath but she knew he could feel the slamming pulse at her wrist and she could see the tension tightening his features too.

He wanted and he would have. Because she wanted too. And maybe this 'want' would have to do. Maybe they could make this work. With the reluctant acceptance of her brother, with the physical attraction binding them, with the baby…maybe this could work *indefinitely*.

She paused at the top of the staircase, drawing in a deeper breath to try to steady her anticipation. Damon released her hand, only to swing her into his arms.

'What are you doing?' she whisper-shrieked, clutching his shoulders as he suddenly strode down the last corridor to her apartment. 'You're not carrying me over my own threshold?'

'Indulge me.'

Excitement rippled down her spine, feathering goosebumps across her skin at his intensity. 'I didn't think you'd be one for wedding traditions.' Her throat felt raspy as she tried to tease.

His grip on her tightened for a nanosecond, and then eased again.

'I was never getting married,' he said carelessly as he kicked the door shut behind them. 'But seeing as that vow has been torn up, I might as well make the most of it.'

She looked into his face as he set her down, wishing she could read his mind. 'Why didn't you want to marry?'

He hesitated for a split second. 'It's not in our nature to be with one person all our lives.'

Our nature, or just *his*? His warning stabbed deep, bursting the warm bubble of desire.

'You don't believe in monogamy?' she clarified, his harsh reality cooling her completely.

'No. I don't.'

So he would cheat on her.

He caught her shoulders, preventing her from walking away from him. 'I think it traps people into a perceived perfection that can't be maintained,' he said quietly, forcing her to meet his gaze. 'No one is infallible, Eleni. Certainly not me. Definitely not you.'

'I can control myself.' Rebellious anger scorched her skin. 'And I intend to keep the vows we just made.'

He smiled. 'Of course you do. And so do I. Until the time when we dissolve the deal. It is just a contract, Eleni. Nothing more.'

Her deeply ingrained sense of tradition and honour railed against that declaration. She'd stood in that chapel and she'd meant those vows. But for Damon, this was nothing more than a business proposition. So why had he carried her only a minute ago?

'But it is a contract with particular benefits,' he added.

'And you intend to make the most of those benefits?' She wasn't buying it.

'As much as you do. Or are you going to try to deny yourself because I've annoyed you?' His smile was all disbelief.

'I'm going to deny *you*.' This might be her wedding night but it made no difference. She wasn't sleeping with him now.

'I've made you angry.' His eyebrows lifted. 'You're very young, sweetheart.'

'No. You're very cynical.' She shoved his chest, but he only took two paces back from her. 'And I'm *not* a child.

Just because I haven't slept with half the world, doesn't mean I'm more stupid than you. Sex doesn't make you smarter. If anything it makes you more dense.'

'Come here, Eleni.'

What, he was going to ignore her argument and simply demand her submission just because he knew she found him sexy?

'Get over yourself.'

'You're saying no?' he asked, his early anger giving way to arrogant amusement. 'Because you're the one used to giving orders?'

'No, that's my brother,' she answered in annoyance. 'I'm the one used to standing in the corner doing what she's told.'

'Then why aren't you doing as you're told now?' He stood with his legs wide like some implacable pirate captain. 'Come here.'

The entrance vestibule of her apartment wasn't huge but it might as well have been the Grand Canyon between them.

'You come over here,' she dared, ignoring the pull of his attraction. 'I'm tired of being told what to do. I'm doing the telling this time.'

His eyes widened fractionally. For a long moment he regarded her silently. She could see the storm brewing in him and braced. Him walking closer was what she wanted. And what she didn't want.

'I'm not yours to boss around or *control*,' she said, touching her tongue to her suddenly dry lips but determinedly maintaining her bravado regardless. 'I'm going to do what's necessary. And *only* what is necessary.'

He took those two paces to invade her personal space again and swept his hand from her waist to her hip. 'This is necessary, Eleni.'

She turned her head away, her heart pounding. 'Not any more.'

'Because you're mad with me.' His lips brushed her cheek. 'Because I've ruined your belief in fairy tales?

There's only the real world, Eleni. With real complications and real mess.'

'And temporary desires,' she ended the lecture for him.

'That's right.'

'And you're feeling a temporary desire now?' she asked.

'Definitely.'

'Too bad.' She clamped her mouth shut.

He laughed again. 'You say you don't play games.' He gifted her the lightest of kisses. 'Say yes to me again, Eleni,' he coaxed, teasing too-gentle hands up and down her spine. 'Say yes.'

She glared at him for as long as she could but she already knew she'd lost. 'You're not fair.'

'Life isn't fair. I thought you knew that already.' He moved closer still, forcing her to step backwards until she was pressed hard between him and the wall. 'Say yes.'

She could hold out but it would only be for a little while. She wanted him too much. She had from the second she'd seen him that night. And it was just sex, right? Nothing to take too seriously. She might as well get something she wanted from this 'contract'.

'Yes.' It was always going to be yes.

His smile was triumphant but she swore she saw tenderness there too. Except it couldn't be that—he'd just told her this was only temporary. He brushed a loose tendril of hair back from her face.

'Don't pet me like I'm a good dog,' she snapped.

He laughed. 'Definitely not a dog. But very good. And very worth petting.' He put hands on her shoulders and applied firm pressure. 'Turn around.'

She met his gaze and sucked in a breath at the fire in his eyes. Wordlessly she let him turn her, surrendering this once.

'This dress is beautiful,' he said softly. 'But not as beautiful as the woman inside it.'

Eleni bowed her head, resting her forehead on the cool

wall. He undid the first button and pressed his lips to the tiny patch of bared skin. His fingers traced, then teased down to the next button. In only a heartbeat Eleni was lost in the eroticism—of not seeing him, but of feeling him expose her to his gaze, to his touch, to his tongue again, inch by slow inch.

Desire unfurled from low in her belly. Her body cared not for the complications and confusion of her heart and mind. Her body cared only for his touch, only for the completion he could bring her.

He teased too much. Too slow. Until she was trembling and breathless.

When her dress slithered to the floor in a rush he put firm hands on her waist and spun her to face him again. She'd worn no bra beneath the gown, so she was left with lacy panties, stockings, kitten heels and nothing else. His gaze was hot and suddenly she was galvanised, reaching out to push him to recklessness again. She wanted him as breathless, as naked—she needed to feel his skin against hers.

But she couldn't undo his buttons. She was too desperate for release from the tension that soared with every second she spent with him. His choked laugh was strained and he took over, swiftly discarding the remainder of his clothes until they lay in a tumble at their feet. For a second she just stared at him. And he at her.

Before she could think, let alone speak, he pulled her close again, as if he couldn't stand to be parted from her for a second longer. He devoured her—with his gaze, then his fingers, then his mouth. He kissed every exposed inch. Somehow they were on the floor and he was braced above her—heavy and strong and dominant. She gasped breathlessly, aching for him. But just at that moment, he lifted slightly away and she almost screamed in protest.

'What?' she snapped at him. Why was he stopping *now*? His smile was both smug and twisted. 'I've had numerous lovers, Eleni, but you're the first one to run away afterwards.'

'Did I hurt your ego?' She half hoped so; that'd be payback for what he was doing to her now.

'You frustrated me. You still do.' A seriousness stole into his features. 'You know I don't want to hurt you.'

She understood frustration now. 'I'm not afraid.'

And he wasn't going to hurt her—he'd made it very clear that this was only this. Only lust. Only temporary.

'No?' He held fast above her. *So close.* 'You're not going to run away again?'

'Not while I'm this naked.' She sighed, surrendering to his seriousness. 'I can handle you.'

'Then no more hiding either,' he ordered, cupping her cheek. 'In this, hold nothing back.'

She was lost in the blue of his intense eyes. He wanted it all his way—acceptance that this was only sex. But at the same time he wanted everything from her. It wasn't fair. But it was life. And it was just them again.

'Okay.' She breathed. A wave of pleasure rolled over her as she accepted his terms. This total intimacy was finally okay.

Less than a second later he drove deep into her body. She cried out as he claimed her with that one powerful thrust. Trembling, she wrapped her arms around his muscular body. Maybe she couldn't handle him. She couldn't cope with how completely he took her, or how exquisitely he now tortured her by just holding still—his invasion total.

'Easy...' he muttered.

There was no easy. 'Please,' she begged, trying to rock her hips beneath him to rouse him into action. 'Please.'

She needed him to move—to take her hard and fast and break the terrible tension gripping her. Because this was too, too good and she was going insane with the desire for release.

'Damn it, Eleni.' He growled and rose on his hands, grinding impossibly deeper.

Passion washed over her. It felt so good she all but lost her mind in the fire that burned out of control so quickly. She was like dry tinder. With one spark the inferno licked to the bone. But suddenly, blessedly, he flared too. Ferociously he rode her. She moaned with every panting short breath until they bucked in unison. Waves of ecstasy radiated through each cell in her body with every one of his forceful thrusts. Fierce and fast she arched, taut and tight around him.

'Eleni.'

She loved the way he ground her name through his clenched teeth. Over and over he stroked her. She clenched her fists as the shuddering rush of pleasure started. Gasping for breath, she revelled in the floods of release as he shouted and thrust hard that one last time, pressing her flat against the wooden floor.

Her emotions surged as the waves of her orgasm ebbed. It was shocking how good he made her feel. How *shattered*. She didn't think she could possibly find the energy to stand, let alone smile. And she wanted to smile. More than that, she wanted him again. Already. She struggled to catch her breath before it quickened, but there was no reining in the rapacious desire that he'd unleashed within her. Only then she felt him moving—away.

Damon winced. Every muscle felt feeble. He'd meant to go more gently and ensure she was with him every step of the way. Hell, he'd meant to make her come first and more than once. But she'd provoked him, and he'd wanted her too much, until he'd taken her like this on the floor— unstoppable and unrestrained and so damn quick all over again.

He rolled onto his side to see more of her lithe, passion-slick, sated body. And this time she turned her head to look back at him. Letting him see her. Her green-blue eyes were luminous. His mouth dried as he read the craving within them. For all his teasing, he understood how much she wanted this. As much as he did. Something shifted inside—a warning that this was far too intense. But it was too late.

If he was any kind of a good guy he'd have wed her and then left her right alone, because, as he'd told her, sleeping together again would lead to complication and she was so inexperienced he didn't want to mess with her emotions. But he wasn't a good guy.

Not a prince, remember?

Fortunately he'd recovered from the whim to carry her into the apartment. That action had turned her soft skin pink, so he'd had to remind her of the reality of their situation. His words had snuffed the starry-eyed look from her face. Now all that remained was the flush of raw desire. Because that was all this was. Romance wasn't real. Love didn't last.

So, better him to be doing this with her than some other jerk, right? At least he was the one she wanted.

He was determined to please her. The sound of her sighs and the fierce heat of her hold were his ultimate reward. The intensity of their chemistry both angered and enthralled him. Now his exhausted body roared with renewed energy. He scooped her into his arms and stood. He'd ached to have her this close. To have her unable to say no to him, wanting and welcoming him—and only him.

He walked through the ornate lounge room, going on instinct to find her bedroom—a surprisingly simply decorated room. He was just so glad to see the bed. He placed her in the centre of it, gritting back the primal growl of victory. His skin tightened as his muscles bunched. Now they'd solved the problem of their immediate future, they could thrash this attraction that burned between them. An understanding of pleasure was the one thing he could give her. The enjoyment of what their bodies were built for, with no shame, no reticence and no regret. Just passion and play.

Satisfaction oozed as he started to tease that wild response from her again. He loved finally having her on the bed with all the time in the world to explore her properly. Her cheeks flushed, her eyes gleamed—dazed, passionate, willing.

He'd had her. He'd have her again. But something ached—something that was missing despite the almost intolerable ecstasy of the last orgasm they'd shared.

'Eleni.' He uttered a plea he hadn't meant to let free.

He'd coerced her into this marriage, but while she'd finally agreed—and accepted that it was only a contract—somehow he wasn't appeased. Not yet. Not even when he made her writhe uncontrollably. Not when she moaned again or when her hands sought to hurry him. Because he refused to be hurried. Not this time. He was slow and deliberate and determined to touch and taste and tease every last inch of her. But even when he'd done that, the nagging gap still irked.

Finally he allowed himself to invade her body with his own again. Helplessly groaning at the unbearable bliss, he locked into place. The driving need to get closer consumed him. He craved her heated softness and tight strength.

'Eleni.' He strained to stay in control.

'Yes.' Her sweet answer rasped over his desire-whipped skin and he drove deeper into her fire. Every muscle tensed as he fought the urge to give in already.

Too soon. It was too soon.

'Damon.' She tracked teasing fingers down his chest until he caught her hand and held it close and she whispered again. Sheer lust vocalised. 'Damon.'

His heart pounded. That was what he wanted. His name on her lips. Her eyes on his. Her body drinking his in. Her whole focus only on him. She arched, willing and sultry, and suddenly her enchanting smile was broken by her release.

'Damon!'

His name. *Screamed.*

A torrent of triumphant energy sluiced through every cell as the last vestige of his self-control snapped. He could no longer hold back, growling his passion as he furiously pounded his way closer. To her. To bliss. His world blackened as rapture hit and satisfaction thundered.

He had won.

CHAPTER TEN

DAMON QUIETLY PACED about the lounge in Eleni's apartment within the palace. His bags had been delivered before the ceremony yesterday and he drew out his tablet now.

The number of emails in his inbox was insane even for him and it wasn't yet eight in the morning. He clicked the first few open and grimaced at the capital letters screaming *CONGRATULATIONS!* at him.

Rattled, he flicked on the television, muting the volume so he couldn't hear the over-excited, high-pitched squeals of the presenters as they gushed about the surprise nuptials of Princess Eleni. A ticker ran along the bottom of the screen repeating the amazing news that she'd married a commoner—one Mr Damon Gale.

The piece they then played was about him. His business interests got a brief mention while his personal ones were explored in depth and all but invented. They focused on his upbringing, his family, his illegitimate half-sister...

He winced when he saw the media crews camped outside Kassie's small apartment in the village. But the horror show worsened in a heartbeat as his father flashed on the screen. Damon automatically iced his emotions—the response had taken him years to perfect. But the sensation of impending doom increased and he flicked on the audio to hear his father in action. Apparently John Gale was 'thrilled' that Eleni and his son Damon's relationship was finally public. His father didn't use her title as he talked, implying intimacy—as if he'd ever met her? But he wasn't afraid of using anyone to push himself further up the slippery pole of success; Damon knew that all too well.

He could hear his father's avaricious glee at the coup
his son had scored.

'You must be very proud of Damon,' one reporter yelled.

His father visibly puffed up. 'Damon is brilliant. He in-
herited his mother's brains.'

Damon gritted his teeth. His father's false praise poked
a wound that should have long healed. His parents were
anything but normal. Narcissistic and concerned only with
image, neither had hearts. Truth be told, nor did he. That
was his genetic inheritance. No capacity for love. No capacity for shame. All his parents had was ambition. He
had that too.

But he'd learned to define his own success. To make it
alone, be the one in control, be the boss. His parents had
been uninterested and absent at best, and abusive at worst,
and they'd taught him well. Yeah, now he had the burning
ambition not to need them or *anyone*.

'What about your daughter, Kasiani?' Another reporter
jostled to the front. 'Is she also a friend of Princess Eleni's?'

His father didn't bat an eyelid at the mention of the
daughter he hadn't seen in years and the reference to the
women that he'd abandoned entirely—not just emotionally,
but financially as well. Damon had actually been jealous
of Kassie until he'd learned his father was truly fickle and
incapable of any kind of decent emotion.

'I really can't comment further on Eleni's personal relationships.' He didn't need to comment further when the
smug satisfaction was written all over his face.

Damon watched as his father walked past the reporter.
But as the cameraman swung the camera to keep filming,
Damon realised just where the interview had taken place—
outside the terminal at Palisades airport.

Which meant his father was here. Now.

Damon muted the sound on the screen and strode from

Eleni's private apartment. He needed to speak to the palace secretary immediately.

'Mr Gale.'

Damon stopped mid-stride down the hallway as Giorgos's private secretary called to him.

'It's your father,' the secretary added.

'Please take me to him,' Damon said quietly.

John Gale had been shown to one of the smaller meeting rooms very near the entrance of the palace. Damon's appreciation of Giorgos's secretary increased and he nodded at the man as he stood back respectfully.

Drawing in a breath, Damon closed the door and faced the father he hadn't seen in five years. Not much had changed. Perhaps he had a little more grey in his hair, a few lines around his eyes, but he still wore that surface-only smile, neat suit and non-stick demeanour.

Damon didn't take a seat, didn't offer one to his father. 'Why are you here?'

'I wanted to congratulate you in person.'

The bare nerve of the man was galling.

'You're very quick off the mark. I haven't been married twenty-four hours yet.'

His father's smile stayed crocodile wide. 'I never thought you had it in you.'

'Had what in me?'

'To marry so…happily.'

'Happily?' Damon queried. 'You mean like you and Mother?'

'Your mother and I have a very successful arrangement.'

Yeah. An arrangement that was bloodless and only about making the most of their assets. 'And that's what you think this is?'

'Are you saying you're in love with her?' His father laughed. 'I'm sure you love the power and opportunity that come with her beautiful body.'

Revulsion triggered rage but Damon breathed deeply,

settling his pulse. He wasn't going to bite. His father wasn't worth it. But he couldn't help declaring the obvious. 'I'm not like you.'

His father frowned. 'Meaning?'

'You have at least one other child that you have done nothing for. You abuse people, then abandon them.'

His father's expression narrowed.

'How many others are there?' Damon asked bluntly.

'That was one mistake.'

Mistake?

'I saw you with her,' Damon said softly, knowing he'd regret the revelation but unable to resist asking.

'Who?'

'Kassie's mother.' Damon had followed him once, here in Palisades—the opulent island of personal betrayal had taken Damon on a swift bleak journey to adulthood and understanding. He'd seen his father kiss that woman with such passion. Damon had actually thought his father was truly in love. That he was truly capable of it and it was just that he didn't feel it for either Damon or his mother. 'Why didn't you leave us and stay with her?' He'd never understood it.

An appalled expression carved deeper lines in his father's face. 'I would never leave your mother.'

'Not because you love her,' Damon said. 'But because her connections were too important to your career. It was your arrangement.'

Because he was that calculating. That ruthlessly ambitious. That incapable of real love.

'Your mother and I make a good team. We understand each other.'

By turning blind eyes to infidelities and focusing on their careers. They'd used his funds and her family name. Connections and money made for progress in political circles. They'd had Damon only to cement the image of the 'perfect career couple'. Not because he'd actually been wanted, as his mother had told him every time he'd disappointed her. And that had been often.

'So you abandoned your lover and your daughter and refused to help when they were struggling because of the risk to your stupid career and supposedly perfect marriage.' Damon was disgusted.

'I offered her money but she was too proud to accept it. That was her choice.'

'You knew she suffered and you didn't go back.'

'What more could I have done, Damon?' his father asked. 'Was it my fault she chose to remain in that squalid little cottage?'

Damon understood it now—he'd realised the horrific truth when he'd learned how that woman had suffered for so long, so alone. His father had never loved Kassie's mother. He'd wanted her, used her and walked away when he'd had enough. When she'd refused his money his conscience was cleared and he'd considered himself absolved.

No guilt. No shame. No heart.

'It'll look strange if you don't invite us both here soon,' his father said, his callousness towards Kassie and her mother apparently forgotten already. 'Your mother would like to stay as a guest.'

'I'm never inviting either of you here,' Damon said shortly. 'How can you act as if we're close when we haven't seen each other in years?' Bitterness burned up his throat. He wanted the taint of the man nowhere near Eleni.

'We've all been busy.'

His father hadn't realised he'd been avoiding him? 'No. We have no relationship. You're not using this. You're not using me.'

'You can't get away from your blood, Damon.' John Gale laughed. 'You're my son. Just because we're more alike than you want to admit, doesn't mean it isn't so. You can't get away from who you are.'

He'd never wanted to be like either of his parents. They

were why he'd never wanted a serious relationship, let alone to marry. Why he'd wanted to build his company—his success—on his own terms. In isolation and not dependent on manipulated relationships.

'I might not be able to deny my blood, but I can deny you access to my wife and to our home,' Damon said coldly. 'You're not welcome here. You'll never be welcome here. I suggest you leave right now, before I have the soldiers throw you out.'

'Your wife's soldiers.'

'Yes.' Damon refused to let his father get a rise out of him. 'Don't come back. Don't contact me again. And don't dare try to contact Eleni directly.'

'Or?'

'Or I'll let the world know just *what* you are.' He'd strike where his father cared the most—his reputation, his image.

John's eyes narrowed.

'It will be much better for you to return to New York and whatever project it is you're about to launch,' Damon said lazily. 'And no more gleeful interviews mentioning Eleni and me. You're showing your lack of class.'

That blow landed and Damon watched as his father's complexion turned ruddy. After that, John didn't stick around and Damon slowly wound his way back up to Eleni's apartment. He'd done the right thing getting him out of the palace as quickly as possible. But his father's slimy insincerity stuck.

He didn't want it getting to Eleni. As soon as the baby was born he'd begin the separation process because she'd be so much better off without him. But he'd still be the Princess's ex-husband, the father of her child. Another prince or princess.

Too late he realised her life was now intrinsically tied to his. His gut tightened as he mulled the possible configurations of their futures and the fact that she would always be part of his world. In the cold light of day he realised he'd not 'won' anything at all.

Nor had she.

But he'd meant what he'd told her. Relationships never lasted. Not for anyone. And certainly not him. Never him. He refused.

He paused for a moment outside her apartment door to draw in a breath. Then he let himself in. It was too much to hope she was still in bed. She was dressed in a simple tee shirt and skirt and his wayward body tightened at the sight of her lithe legs.

'Where have you been?' she asked, sending him a sleepy smile, but her sea-green eyes were too searching for him to cope with.

'I have a company to run,' Damon said sharply, picking up his tablet and staring at it. Hard. 'I've neglected it long enough while tracking you down.'

Silence filled the room, tightening the invisible string connecting his eyes to her body and in the end he could no longer resist the tug.

A limpid look was trained on him. 'Perhaps you should have slept a little longer.'

He couldn't help but smile at that most princess-polite sass.

She wandered over to the window, affording him an even better view of her legs and the curve of her body. She had no idea of her sensuality.

'So what have you been working on that's caused your mood to…deteriorate?'

'It's not important.'

'It wouldn't have anything to do with your father, would it?'

He froze. 'Your palace spies have reported in already?'

'No spies. I saw a replay of the interview with him at the airport.' She turned to face him. 'Is he here?'

'He's already left.'

'You didn't want me to meet him?'

'No.' He didn't want to explain why. But he saw the wounded flash in her eyes. 'He's not a nice man.'

Her lips twisted. 'You don't need to protect me.'

'Yes, I do.' He huffed out a breath and glared at his tablet again, gripping it as if it were his life-support system.

His marriage to Eleni could be nothing like his parents' one. For one thing, it wasn't about to last. It wasn't about his career and never would be. It was about protecting his child. It was about protecting Eleni.

'Are you sure it's me you're protecting?' she asked quietly.

He glanced across at her. 'Meaning?'

'Your father...and you.' She looked uncomfortable. 'You're not close...'

'No.' Damon couldn't help but smile faintly. Definitely not close. 'I haven't had contact with him in almost five years.'

'None at all?'

He shook his head.

'He cheated on your mother.' She still looked super awkward. 'Kassie at the hospital...'

'Is my unacknowledged half-sister. Yes.'

'But you're in touch with her.'

'Yes.' He sighed and put the tablet down on the low table. 'My father isn't. My mother pretends she doesn't exist. Kassie is too proud to push for what she's owed.' He leaned back on the edge of the sofa, folding his arms across his chest. He'd had to find out what had happened. 'I once saw him with her mother,' Damon said. 'Years ago when we lived here in Palisades.'

'That must have been hard to see.'

Damon frowned at the floor. 'I couldn't understand why he didn't leave us for them when it was so obvious...'

'Did you ever ask him?'

About five minutes ago and his father had confirmed

what Damon had learned in later years. 'His career was too important. It was always too important to both my parents. The only reason they had me was to tick that box on their CV—happily married with one son...'

'But they must be proud of you.'

He laughed bitterly. 'Proud of a teenager who wasted his time making lame computer games?' He shook his head.

'But now you have a hugely successful company. More than one. How can they not be—?' She broke off and her expression softened. 'You shouldn't have had to "achieve" to get the support any child deserves.'

'I got more than my half-sister did,' he muttered shortly. 'He wouldn't even support them financially. Her mother died a long, slow, painful death. Kassie has been struggling since.'

'Is that why you got in touch with her?'

He nodded. 'But she wouldn't let me help her.' He rolled his shoulders. It still knotted him that Kassie had refused almost everything he'd offered. 'I can understand it.'

Sadness lent a sheen to Eleni's eyes. 'And your parents are still together.'

'Still achieving. Still silently seething with bitterness and unhappiness. Still a successful marriage. Sure thing.'

'He cheated more than once?'

'I expect so,' he sighed.

'So.' Eleni brushed her hair back from her face. 'That's why you made it clear our marriage is only to provide legitimacy for our baby. Why you think no relationship lasts.'

'As I said, a child shouldn't be raised in the household with unhappily married parents.' Unloving parents. 'We married for the birth certificate, then we do what's right. I didn't want this baby to be a tool for some political purpose. Not paraded as the future Prince or Princess or whatever. And I won't abandon it either.'

'I understand,' she said softly. 'I don't want that either.'

She bit her lip and looked down at the table between them. 'I'm sorry your parents…'

He held up a hand. 'It's okay. We all have our burdens, right?' She'd lost both her parents. She had expectations on her that were far beyond the normal person's. He shouldn't have judged her as harshly as he had.

'Damon?'

He glanced up at that roughened note in her voice.

Storms had gathered in her sea-green eyes. 'This baby was unexpected, unplanned…' she pressed a hand to her flat belly as she gazed across at him '…but I promise you I'll love it. I already do. I'll do whatever it takes to protect and care for it.'

'I know.' He believed her because she already was. He'd seen her stand up to her brother—knew that had been a first for her. And she was trying here, now, with him.

But somehow it made that discomfort within him worse. He wasn't like her. He didn't understand how she could love the child already. The truth was he didn't know how to love. He had no idea how to be a husband. He sure as hell had no idea how to be a father. When he'd first suspected she might be pregnant his initial instinct had been not to abandon his child. He was not doing what his father had done to Kassie.

But he had no idea how even these next few months were going to work. The tightness in his chest didn't ease. Disappointment flowed and then ebbed. Leaving him with that *void*. He ached for a real escape.

'Is that the photo Giorgos approved for release?' Eleni's voice rose in surprise.

He glanced at the muted screen still showing the number one news item of the world.

'Yes.' He cleared his throat. 'There's another with him in it as well, but this is the one the media have run with.'

'I can't believe he chose that one. It's…'

'What?'

'Informal.'

Damon knew why the King had chosen that particular picture. Eleni looked stunning with her skin glowing, her hair and dress beautiful...but it was that luminosity in her expression that was striking. While Damon was looking at her with undeniable desire, she was laughing up at him—sparkling, warm, delighted. This image, snapped in that moment in the garden, would sell the 'truth' of this fairy tale.

This image stole his breath.

But now another picture of him flashed on the screen—him at an event with another woman. Then another. Inwardly he winced. It seemed anyone who'd dated him in the past wanted their five minutes of fame now and had opened their photo albums to show off their one or two snaps.

'Wow, lots of models, huh?' Eleni muttered, her rasp more apparent. 'That's very billionaire tech entrepreneur of you.'

'It wasn't a deliberate strategy.' He stepped nearer to her, needing to touch her skin. 'They just happened to be at the parties.'

She subjected him to a long, silent scrutiny. 'You know my history. I don't know yours at all.'

'You mean lovers?' He grinned in an effort to shake off the prickling sensation her piercing greenish gaze caused. 'I've had a few. No real girlfriends. There's nothing and no one to trouble you.'

She didn't look convinced.

He shrugged. 'I'm busy with my work and I like to be good at it.'

The ugly fact was he was a hollow man—as success obsessed as his shallow parents. Just less visible about it. He liked to think he had a smidge more integrity than they did—by refusing to use other people to get to where he wanted to be. Utter independence was what he craved.

'Do you know I've got at least twenty new work offers

today purely because of my involvement with you?' he said a little roughly.

She lifted her eyebrows. 'And that isn't good?'

'*I* haven't earned these opportunities, Eleni.'

'Perhaps you could take advantage of them to enable other people to progress as well. To create jobs and other contracts—'

Her naive positivity hit a raw nerve. '*I* built my company from scratch.'

'And you don't want your association with me compromising your success story?' Her cheeks pinked. 'At least you had the choice to forge your own path. I'm one of the most privileged people on the planet and, while I am grateful for that, I'm also bound by the rules that come with it. I couldn't do what I want.'

And it seemed she still couldn't. He grabbed his tablet again and showed her the endless list of invitations and formal appearances the palace official had sent him. 'Is this amount normal?' he asked. 'Which would you usually decline?'

Her eyebrows shot up. 'None.'

None? He paused. 'There are too many requests here.'

Were they were trying to schedule her every waking moment? Damon wasn't having it.

'You don't say no.' The shock on her face said it all.

She really was a total pawn in the palace machine. Well, he wasn't letting them take advantage of Eleni, or her child, or him. Not any more.

'I'm okay with saying no,' he said.

'Well, I don't like to be perceived as lazy.' Her lips tightened. 'Or spoilt.'

And that was why Princess Eleni had always done as she was told—wore what was expected, said what was polite, did what was her duty. She'd obediently played her princess role perfectly for years.

Except when it had come to him. That night with him

she'd done what she *wanted*. She'd taken. And since then? She'd argued. She'd stood up for herself. She'd been everything but obedient when it came to him...

He didn't want that changing because she felt some misguided sense of obligation now she was married to him. Hell, she was likely to want to play the part of the 'perfect wife' but he wasn't letting it happen. For the first time in her life, he wanted Eleni Nicolaides to experience some true freedom.

'Why did you want to stay in Palisades rather than go to Giorgos's safe house in France?' he asked roughly.

She looked down. 'This probably sounds crazy, but it's actually more private here.'

'You're *happy* to be trapped inside the palace walls?'

She shrugged her shoulders. 'It's what I'm used to. I can show you how it works.'

He didn't need to know how it worked. He had a headache from all the gilded decorations already. 'I know somewhere even more private.' He rubbed his shoulder. 'I think we should go there.'

'You don't understand—'

'Yeah, I do. I know about the paparazzi and the press and the cell phones in every member of the public's hands. But my island is safe. It's secure. It's private.'

She stilled. 'Your island?'

She really hadn't done any research on him, had she? That both tickled him, and put him out.

'You have your island, I have mine.' He sent her a sideways grin. 'I'll admit mine isn't as big, but good things come in small packages.'

The look in her eyes was decidedly not limpid now. 'Are you trying to convince me that size doesn't matter?' she teased in that gorgeously raspy voice. 'Of course, I have no basis for comparison, for all I know I might be missing out—'

'You're concerned you're missing out?' He rose to her

bait, happy to slip back into this tease and turn away from the too serious.

'You tell me.' She batted her eyelashes at him.

This was the woman from that night at the ball—that playful, slightly shy, deliciously fun woman.

'Hell, yeah, you're missing out.'

Her mouth fell open.

'Come with me and I'll show you.'

Her lips twisted as colour flowed into her cheeks.

'It's in the Caribbean,' he purred.

She closed her mouth. 'That is also very tech billionaire of you.'

'Yeah. It is. So let's go there. Today.' He stood, energy firing. For the first time since seeing that damn screen this morning he felt good.

'But Giorgos—'

'But Giorgos what? We can let him know where we've gone.' He paused, waiting to see if she'd defy her brother's orders.

A gleam lit in her eye. Damon suppressed his smug smirk—seemed his Princess had unleashed her latent rebellious streak. He liked it.

'How long does it take to get there?'

CHAPTER ELEVEN

ELENI SAT ACROSS from Damon in one of the large leather recliners in his private jet and tried not to stare at him. Her face heated as she recalled what he'd done to her, what he'd encouraged her to do to him. Last night had been the first time she'd ever shared a bed. The first time she'd slept in a man's arms. She couldn't even *remember* falling asleep, only a feeling of supreme relaxation as she'd lain entwined with him.

'It's a long flight. You should rest while you can.' That wicked glint ignited his smile as if he knew exactly what she was thinking about.

'I need rest?'

'For the days ahead, yes.'

'Empty promises…threats…' she muttered softly.

He leaned forward and placed his finger over her lips. 'Don't worry. I'll make good on every one. When we're alone.'

'I see no cabin crew.' She blinked at him.

'You want them to hear you?' His eyebrows arched. 'Because you're not going to be quiet.'

'I can be quiet.'

'Can you?' He studied her intently, not bothering to add anything more.

Heat deepened and spread, heating her from the inside out. Every, single cell. Realisation burned. She was never going to be quiet with him.

'You're…' She couldn't think of her own name, let alone a suitable adjective this second.

'Good.' Looking smug, he leaned back in his seat and pulled his tablet out. 'I'm very good.'

'Full of yourself,' she corrected.

She couldn't sit for hours with nothing to occupy her except sinful thoughts. She burrowed in her bag and fetched out the paper and small pencil tin that she always had stashed. Sketching soothed, like meditation. And she'd spent so many hours with a pencil in hand, it was calming.

He didn't seem to notice her occupation. She became so engrossed in her work she lost track of time. When she glanced up she discovered he'd closed his eyes. She wasn't surprised; he'd had as little sleep as she. And he'd been worryingly pale when he'd returned to her apartment this morning after that meeting with his father.

With that downwards tilt to his sensual lips now, she understood that he was vulnerable too and much more complex than she'd realised. He'd been hurt. His parents' infidelities, their lack of support and interest. Their falseness.

Yet he'd grown strong. Now she understood his fierce independence and the fury he'd felt when he'd thought she'd somehow betrayed him. He didn't trust and she didn't blame him. He only wanted his child to avoid the hurt he'd experienced.

She looked down at the sketch she'd done of him and cringed. She'd never want him to see this—too amateur. Too embarrassing. She folded the paper over and put it in the small bin just as the pilot announced they weren't far from landing. Damon opened his eyes and flashed her a smile.

'It's just a short hop by helicopter from here,' he said as the plane landed.

'That's what you say to everyone you bring here?'

He met her gaze. 'You already know I never brought any of my women here. This is my home.'

'Heaven forbid you'd let any of them get that close.'

'Wouldn't want them getting the wrong idea.'

'I'm glad I "trapped" you into marriage, then, now I get to kick about on your little island.'

Damon grinned at her. Yeah, he couldn't wait for her to kick about. But he held back as Eleni gathered her small bag and stepped ahead of him to exit the plane. He'd seen her discard the drawing she'd been working on and he was too curious to let it go. On his way out he swiftly scooped up the paper and pocketed it. Given she'd been secretive and clearly hadn't wanted him to see it, he was going to have to pick the moment to ask her about it.

The helicopter ride was smooth but wasn't quick enough. He ached to get there—to his home. His own private palace. His peace.

He breathed out as they finally landed and he strode to the open-topped Jeep that he'd ordered to be left waiting for their arrival.

'Let me take you on a tour.' He winked at her. 'You can see exactly what kind of prize husband you've claimed for yourself.'

'You're not the prize. I am,' Eleni answered sassily as she shook her hair loose in the warm sunshine. 'It really is your island?'

'It's the company compound,' he drawled. 'We futuristic tech companies must have amazing work places for our staff. It's part of the image.'

'I didn't think you were a slave to any society's required "image". You're the man who doesn't care what anyone thinks of him, right?'

Right. *Almost.*

Reluctant amusement rippled through him. He liked it when she sparked up.

She stared as the pristine coastline came into clear view. He heard her sharp intake of breath. Now as he drove they could see a few roofs of other dwellings amongst the verdant foliage. He knew it was beautiful, but he was glad she could see it too.

'They live here all year round?'

'No.' He laughed that she'd taken him so seriously. 'It really is just my island. It was a resort, now it's not. My people stay for stints if they need to complete a big project, or to recharge their batteries. Every employee has at least six weeks a year here. Families can come too, of course.' He parked up by the main beach. 'Energy-wise it's self-sufficient, thanks to all the solar-power generation, and we grow as many supplies as we can.'

'So it's paradise.'

'Yeah.' Pure, simple luxury. 'There's no paparazzi. No media. No nosey parkers watching your every move. It is completely private.'

She glanced up into the blindingly blue—clear—sky. 'No drones? No spy cams everywhere?'

'No helicopters. No long-range lenses. No nothing. Just peace and security,' he confirmed, but grimaced wryly. 'And half my staff…but they'll be busy and you can do whatever you want, whenever you want.'

'With whomever I want?' she asked. There was an extra huskiness to her tone that made him so hard.

'No.' He reached across and turned her chin so she faced him. 'Only with me.'

She mock-pouted, teasing in that playful way he adored—demanding retribution of the most erotic kind. But after only a kiss he reluctantly pulled away. He couldn't bring her here and hurry her into bed. He could be more civilised than that.

'Come on,' he said briskly, getting out of the Jeep and pointing to the meandering path through the lush trees. 'I'll show you around the complex.'

Then he'd take her to his house and have her all to himself at last.

Eleni didn't want to blink and miss a moment. His island was like a warm jewel, gleaming with the promise of heat and holiday and indefinable riches. And with that total privacy, it was the ultimate treasure. A feeling of relaxation slowly unfurled through her body, spreading warmth and joy and such anticipation she could hardly contain it.

'This is the "den"—our main office here.'

She followed him into the large building. It was a large open space filled with desks, computers and space for tinkering and was currently occupied by five guys all standing round a giant screen.

'Going from left to right, we have Olly, Harry, Blair, Jerome and Faisal,' Damon said to her in a low voice. 'You have that memorised already, right?'

She smiled because, yes, she had.

'Guys,' Damon called to them. 'I'd like you to meet Eleni.'

Not *Princess*. Not *my wife*. Just Eleni. That different kind of warmth flowed through her veins again.

The men turned and shouts erupted. But not for her. It was pleasure that their boss had returned. One of the guys stepped to the side of the swarm around Damon to greet her.

'Nice to meet you, Eleni.' Olly's accent placed him as Australian.

The other men nodded, smiled and positively pounced on Damon again.

'Look, D—I know you're not here for work, but can I just run a couple things past you?' Faisal asked.

Damon was already halfway across the room, his gaze narrowing at the gobbledegook on the screen. 'Of course.'

All the men perked up but Eleni saw Olly and Jerome exchange a look and a jerk of the head towards her. The next second Jerome walked over.

'Eleni…' Jerome cleared his throat. 'Welcome. You must…ah…'

'I'm really happy to be here.' She smiled to put him at

ease. Eleni could make conversation with anyone. 'What is it you guys are working on?'

He led her to the nearest table that was covered in an assortment of electronics components and plastic figurines. 'We're designing a new visuals prototype and we need his thoughts on the latest version.'

'Visuals prototype?'

To his credit, Jerome spent a good five minutes explaining the tech to her and answering her questions. But it was obvious he was eager to talk to Damon too and in the end she put him out of his misery. 'Go ask him whatever it is you need to. I'm fine,' she laughed.

'Are you sure?' Jerome looked anxiously between her and Damon.

'Of course.'

He hurried away to join the conference around the screen. Damon stood in the centre, listening intently then quietly offering his opinion. The Australian was making notes on a piece of paper while Harry asked another question prompting another concise answer. It was evident they valued his every word and had missed his input. Everyone in the vicinity was paying total attention—to him. Eleni gradually became aware she was staring at him too. And for once no one was staring at *her*.

Blushing, she turned away and stepped outside to take in some fresh air. Her muscles ached slightly and a gentle feeling of fatigue made her sleepy. She leaned against the tall tree just outside the building and looked across at the beautifully clear water.

Ten minutes later Damon walked back to where she waited in the shade.

'Sorry,' he muttered as he reached to take her hand. 'That took longer than I realised.'

'It's fine. I enjoyed looking around.'

Damon sent her a speculative look that turned increasingly wicked the longer he studied her. 'What have you been thinking about?' he asked. 'You've gone very pink.'

The heat in her cheeks burned. 'Don't tease.'

'Oh, I'll tease.' He tugged on her hand and pulled her closer to him. 'But first let me show you the rest.'

'I think rest is a good idea.' She wanted to be alone with his undivided attention on *her* again. And right now she didn't care if that made her spoiled.

'There's a restaurant room,' he said.

Of course there was. Right on the beach, with a bar and a woman who waved and smiled at Damon the second she saw him. Eleni's spine prickled.

'Rosa will cook anything you want, as long as you want fresh and delicious.' Damon waved at the relaxed, gorgeously tanned woman and kept walking past.

'This place is just beautiful.' Eleni glanced back at the restaurant.

'Rosa is married to Olly, the guy with—'

'The beard.' Eleni sighed, stupidly relieved. 'The Australian.'

Damon grinned as if he'd sensed her irrational jealous flare. 'They live here most of the year round.'

'Lucky them.' She walked across the sand with him. 'Do you live here most of the year too?'

'Meetings take me away, but I'm here when I can be.'

Eleni could understand why; if it were her choice she'd never leave. But his marriage to her was going to make that problematic for a while. She had duties in Palisades that she had to perform.

'Where next?' she asked. 'Your house?'

'Not yet. You haven't seen the playroom.'

'Playroom?' she asked, startled.

He laughed and gave her a playful swipe. 'Not *that* kind of playroom.' He cocked his head. 'But now I know you're curious…'

'Shut it and show me the room.' She marched across the sand, cheeks burning.

It was a boat shed and it was filled with every water-sport toy imaginable—from surfboards, to kayaks to inflatables and jet skis. 'Okay, this is seriously cool.' She stepped forward to get a closer look.

'I knew you liked the water,' Damon said smugly. 'You swim, right?'

'Indoors at the palace,' she answered, checking out the kayaks stacked in racks up the wall. 'Giorgos had a resistance current feature installed so I can train each morning in privacy.'

'You don't swim in the sea?'

'With everyone watching?' She stared at him as if he were crazy. 'Rating my swimsuits every morning?' She shook her head. 'And he'd never let me on a jet ski.'

'No?' Damon's eyes widened.

'Safety issues.' She shrugged and straightened. 'And again, too many photographers.'

'You like to avoid those.'

'Do you blame me?'

'No.' He leaned against the door frame and sent her a smouldering look. 'I'm really good on a jet ski,' he said arrogantly. 'You can come with me.'

She crossed her arms and sent what she hoped was a smouldering look right back at him. 'Can I drive?'

'Sure. I have no problem with that.'

'But what if I want to go fast?' She blinked at him innocently.

'I think I can keep up.' He lifted away from the door frame and strolled towards her.

'You think?' Her voice rose as he stepped close enough to pull her against him.

'I think it's time you saw my house,' he growled.

'It's beyond time,' she whispered.

He guided her across the sand and up a beautifully maintained path through the well-established trees to the gorgeous building at the end.

An infinity pool—the perfect length for laps—was the feature at the front. Comfortable, beautiful furniture was strategically placed to create space for relaxation, conversation and privacy. The house itself was wooden, with two storeys, and not monstrously huge but nor was it small. Damon didn't speak as he led her inside—he simply let her look around. It was luxurious, yes, but also cosy with a sense of true intimacy. She didn't know why that surprised her, but it did.

He still said nothing, but smiled as if he sensed her appreciation. She took his outstretched hand and he led her up the curling wooden staircase. She assumed it led to his bedroom. Her heart hammered. A delicious languorous anticipation seeped into her bones.

But while there were doors to other rooms on one side, the room he drew her to wasn't for sleeping. It stretched the length of the building. Unsurprisingly it was dominated by symmetrical windows overlooking the sand, sea and sky. A long table took up half the space. It was clearly his desk, given the neatly stacked piles of papers and the writing utensils gathered in a chipped mug. A long seat took up much of the remaining window space. A single armchair stood in front of the large fireplace that broke up the floor-to-ceiling bookshelves that covered the wall opposite the windows. Books were stacked on every shelf. Books that had clearly been read and weren't just there for the look of it. This was more than his workspace. It was his think space—his escape.

'I can see why you love it.' She stood in the middle of the room and gazed from the intriguing space inside to the natural beauty outside.

'Best view on the island.'

'The beauty is more than the view.' She noted the shades for the windows, the pale warmth of the walls, the art that he'd chosen to complement the space. 'The light is lovely,' she said softly. 'The colour. It must help you focus.'

'It's not a palace,' he said with a keen look.

'It's better than any palace.'

A small smile flitted about his mouth. 'So you like it?'

Intrigued that her opinion genuinely seemed to matter, she turned her back on the view to face him directly. 'Did you honestly think I wouldn't?' She wasn't that spoilt, was she?

'There's not a lot of gold leaf and crystal chandeliers.'

'Did you think I wasn't going to like it because there's no ballroom?' She felt slightly hurt. 'You don't need a ballroom—you have a beach.' She looked out across the water again. 'You're lucky to have a home, not a museum in which you live.'

She and Giorgos didn't own the palace, they were the guardians for the future of it, and for the people of Palisades. This small island was utterly Damon's and she had to admit she was a little jealous.

'You can stay here any time,' he said.

She sent him a crooked smile, rueful that he'd so clearly read her mind. She didn't want to think about the future yet. She just wanted to enjoy this freedom, in this moment. Enjoy him, while she had him.

'Thank you.' She faced him, determined to take the initiative, despite the mounting burn in her cheeks. 'So may I sit in the driver's seat?'

His focus on her sharpened. 'Meaning?'

Silently she just looked at him. He knew exactly what she meant already.

'Tell me,' he said softly—a combination of demand and dare. 'You can tell me anything.'

His easy invitation summoned that streak of boldness within her, just as it had that very first night. Something in him gave her the courage to claim what she wanted. The courage she got only with him. Only for him.

'I want to kiss you,' she muttered huskily and swallowed before continuing. 'The way you've kissed me.'

He stared at her so intently she wondered if he'd turned to stone.

'I dare you to let me,' she whispered.

'Is this what you've been thinking about?'

'All day,' she admitted with a slow nod.

His smile was as rueful—and as honest—as hers had been only moments earlier. He lifted his hands in a small gesture of surrender. 'That's why you drew this?' He held up a piece of paper.

She winced as she saw what he was holding. 'I put that in the rubbish.'

'Which was a shame.'

That he'd seen that drawing was the most embarrassing thing. Because it was him. Half nude. Heat flooded her. Mortifying, blistering heat.

'Why didn't you study Fine Arts?' he asked.

'It would have been arrogant to assume I had talent.' She hadn't been allowed.

'You do have talent.'

His words lit a different glow in her chest but she laughed it off. 'You're just flattered because I gave you abs.'

'I do have abs.'

'I don't usually draw...' She couldn't even admit it.

'Erotic pictures?' He laughed. 'What do you usually draw?'

'Dogs,' she said tartly.

'The pictures in Kassie's ward at the hospital are yours, right? You draw them for the children.'

He'd seen those? 'They're just doodles.' She shrugged it off.

'You're talented, Eleni.'

'You're very kind.' She bent her head.

He gripped her arms and made her look at him again.

'Don't go "polite princess" on me. Accept the compliment for what it is—honest.'

That fiery heat bloomed in her face again.

'Do you paint as well?'

'Sometimes, but mostly pen and ink drawings.'

'You're good, Eleni.'

'You promised me you were good,' she whispered.

A smile sparked in his eyes but he shook his head. 'You're trying to distract me.'

'Is it working?'

'You know it is. But why can't you take the compliment?'

Because it was too intimate. Too real. It meant too much. His opinion of her shouldn't matter as much as it did. But she didn't say any of that. She just shrugged.

'You have a lot to offer the world,' he said softly.

For a moment it was there again—that flicker of intensity that was different from the pure desire that pulled them together in the first place. This was something deeper. Something impossibly stronger. And she backed away from it.

'Stop with the flattery or I'll never leave,' she joked.

There was a moment of silence and she couldn't look at him.

'Where will you have me?' With those husky words he let her lead them back into that purely sensual tease. The easier, safer option.

'Here. Now.'

She walked, nudging him backwards. All the way to that comfortable armchair. She pushed his chest and he sat. She remained standing, looking down at him. He'd not had the chance to shave since their flight and the light stubble on his jaw lent him a roguish look. That curl to his lips was both arrogant and charming.

She leaned forward. 'Damon,' she breathed as she kissed him.

'Yes.' He held very still beneath her ministrations.

'You're irresistible.' She sent him a laughing look.

He chuckled. 'I'm glad you think so.' He tensed as she slowly undid his buttons. 'What a relief.'

'You don't seem very relieved.'

'I'm trying to stay in control.'

'Why would you want to do that?'

'I don't want to scare you.'

She laughed. 'You're no ogre.'

'I don't want you to stop,' he whispered.

'Why would I? I want you to lose control. You make me lose control all the time.'

'Eleni…'

'It's only fair,' she muttered. Not teasing.

'Fair? You know that's not how it works.'

A frisson of awareness reverberated through her body. Delight. Desire. Danger. That intensity flickered again. But she moved closer. Took him deeper. Stroked him harder. Doing everything she'd secretly dreamed of doing. She'd show him *not fair*.

He groaned. 'Don't stop.'

Pleased, she kissed him again and then again. His hands swept down her sides, stirring her to the point where she couldn't concentrate any more. She drew back.

'Stop touching,' she growled at him. 'It's my turn.'

He half laughed. She squeezed. Hard.

'Mine,' she said seriously—and for more than just this 'turn'.

He met her gaze. The blue of his eyes deepened as that something passed between them. No matter that she tried to dance past it, it kept curling back—entwining around them.

He lifted a hand, threading his fingers through her hair to cup the nape of her neck. 'Mine.'

His echo was an affirmation, not an argument. He was hers to hold. Hers to have. And yes, she was his too.

For now. Only for now.

She closed her eyes and let herself go—taking exactly what she wanted, touching in the way she'd only dreamed and never before dared. She liked feeling his power beneath her. Liked his vulnerability like this—letting her pleasure him.

'Eleni.'

She felt his power and restraint and fought to topple it. He curled his hands around the armrests and she heard his breathing roughen. His muscles flexed and she tasted salt as sweat slicked his skin.

'Eleni.'

She tightened her grip, swirling her tongue, and simply willed for him to feel it the same way she did—that unspeakable bliss. 'Let me make you feel good.'

That was what he did for her.

Spent and satisfied physically, a different need surged fiercely through Damon. He didn't want her doing this out of gratitude or pity. He lifted her onto his lap and cupping her chin, stared hard into her eyes—heavy-lidded, sea-green storms of desire gazed back at him. Dazed, yet seemingly seeing right into his soul.

Pure instinct drove him. He kissed her, slipping his hand under her skirt, skating his fingers all the way to her secret treasure. His heart seized as he discovered how hot and wet she was and satisfaction drummed in his heart. She'd not gone down on him from a sense of obligation; she'd almost got off on it. The least he could do was help her get the rest of the way. This thing between them had them equally caught. Her need—her ache—was his. Just as his was hers. She moaned as he flicked his fingers and pushed her harder, faster. He kissed her again and again, almost angry in the pleasure and relief of discovering her extreme arousal. It took only a moment and then she was there, pleasure shuddering through her body.

She was inexperienced, yet lustful. Her shy but unashamed sensuality felled him—he wanted to make it better and better for her. But there was no bettering what was already sublime. No beating the chemistry that flared so brightly whenever they came into contact.

He held her in his arms and stood, carrying her down the stairs to the comfort of his bed. In this one thing, at least, he could meet every one of her needs.

Again, again, and again.

CHAPTER TWELVE

'I THINK YOU can go a little faster than that.' Damon double-checked her life vest and then dared her.

'It's even more fun than I imagined.' Eleni smiled at him from astride the jet ski.

He grinned at the double-meaning glint in her eye. With wild hair and without a speck of make-up his Princess was more luminous than ever. With each moment he spent with her, he grew more intrigued. But he forced a laugh past the lump in his throat. 'Because you like fast.'

'I must admit I do.'

'Then why not see if you can beat me.'

Her eyes flashed again and he relished the way she rose to his challenge. He liked seeing her this happy. The one thing he could do was give her more moments of freedom before she returned to full-time royal life and that damn goldfish bowl she lived in.

He got on the other jet ski. 'Come on, we'll go to the cove.'

Her laughter rang out as she took off before he was ready. Grinning, he revved his engine and set out to hunt her down.

Two hours later Eleni sat on the beach suffused with a deep sense of contentment. The place was paradise—and Damon in paradise? Heartbreaking. He talked, teased, laughed. But she liked him like this too—just sitting quietly alongside her, relaxed and simply enjoying the feel of the sun.

Now she understood why he'd been unable to trust her initially. Why he didn't want his child caught between parents knotted together unhappily. But now that she knew, things had changed. Her feelings for him were deepening, growing, causing confusion.

She sat forward as a shiver ran down her spine. She didn't like the cold streak of uncertainty; she'd bring forward warmth instead. She sent him a coy look. 'I think I should go back to the house and have an afternoon nap.'

'Ride with me this time. One of the guys will come get the other jet ski later.'

He sped back to the main beach while she unashamedly clung, loving the feel of the wind on her face and the spray of the sea, taking the chance to rest before what was to come. But when they walked up to the house, he diverted to the staircase, turning to her with a smile on his face.

Eleni stood on the threshold and stared at the new desk that had replaced the window seat in Damon's office. It was angled, an artist's desk. A cabinet stood beside it, together with a folded easel. Boxes of art supplies were neatly stacked on the top of the cabinet and instinctively she knew that were she to open the drawers, she would most likely find more. Paper, paint, pens, pencils, pastels, ink, brushes, canvas—so many art supplies and a desk and chair that were not for Damon to use. But for her.

Her heart raced. 'When did you arrange this?'

Why had he arranged this? She stared at the beautifully set out equipment and then looked at him.

That gorgeous smile curved his mouth but he just shrugged. 'I unleashed one of the graphic designers in an art store in the States. He got in last night and set it up while we were out just now.' His gaze narrowed on her. 'Would it have been better for you to choose the supplies yourself?'

'No. No, this is…amazing. It's so much better than what I use at home.'

He nodded slowly. 'You don't spend money on it because—'

'It's just a hobby,' she answered quickly.

'But it's more than a hobby to you.'

She was unbearably touched that he understood how much she loved it. 'It's not going to bother you that I'm working here?'

Damon's smile faded, leaving him looking sombre, and suddenly that intensity flared between them. That silent pull of something that tried to bind them closer. 'I'm not going to tease you with the obvious answer because this is actually too important.' He reached out and cupped her face. 'I don't want you to sit in the corner and be decorative and silent. I like your company. And not just…'

He let the sentence hang and his smile said it all.

Eleni stared up at him, her own smile tremulous. He'd put her in his space—placed her desk next to his and drawn her close to his side. He wanted her near him. Eleni had never had such a gift.

'Thank you,' she said softly. 'I like your company too.'

When she woke the next morning Damon had already risen. She showered and put on a loose summer dress. She took some toast and fruit from the breakfast tray and climbed the stairs to see him. He glanced up from the book he was reading. In his white tee, beige trousers and bare feet, he was too gorgeous.

Even more so when that roguish smile lit up his eyes. 'I thought you might sleep in.'

Heat burned in her cheeks as she remembered the little sleep they'd stolen through the night. But she was determined to tease him every bit as much as he teased her, so she adopted her most princessy tone.

'I might take a nap later. You may care to join me then.' She gestured at her desk. 'I thought I'd take a look at my new toys, if that's okay.'

He shut his book with a snap and sent her a stern look. 'You ruined it with that last bit. You don't need my permission. You're free to do whatever you want.' He reached for another book on his desk. 'I'm not your King, Eleni. Not your master.'

She knew that. 'I was just trying to be polite.'

'You don't need to try to be anything with me, Eleni. You can just be yourself.'

She was self-conscious to start with, too aware of how near he was and nervous of making too much noise as she removed plastic wrap and opened packets. She'd never really shared space like this with anyone.

'I'm messy,' she said, glancing at the bottles of ink she'd opened to test out. 'Sorry.'

'That's okay. I'm messy too.'

That was a lie; his desk was immaculate. But as the morning progressed, the piles beside him began to grow. He read more than she'd have thought possible. He sent emails in batches, took video calls over the Internet. His focus didn't surprise her, nor his ability to recall facts or tiny facets of design and interface.

Rosa appeared with another tray of food—fresh, beautifully prepared and presented. Eleni was used to immaculate service but this was different. This was more intimate, more relaxed, more friendly. Just like the island itself. He had such privacy and freedom here. It was the perfect holiday escape for her.

But it was his reality. His life. The space he'd secured for himself to think and create and build.

He connected or disconnected from the rest of the world as he pleased. No wonder he'd looked so uncomfortable at the thought of spending serious time in the palace. It wasn't that he couldn't handle it, it was just that he didn't want to. He had other things to think about—fascinating things, much more meaningful to him than gallery openings and charity visits.

And he had history back in Palisades—bitter family history that hurt. She understood that, for him, attendance at glittering events was only to promote the fallacy of his parents' marriage. He thought everything about those evenings was false. But he was wrong.

They did important work. They had value too. She just had to help him understand it.

Lost in thought, she opened the drawers of the cabinet and selected a sheet of paper. She needed this time out to figure out their future. To accept it.

As she settled into her exploration of pen nibs and ink and the tin of beautiful pencils, time snuck away. When light glinted on the glass of water beside her desk, she looked up from the picture she'd fallen into drawing. To her surprise, the sun was almost at its zenith and she knew both the sand and the water would be warm. Her whole body melted at the thought.

'I just need to get this message sent and I'll go with you.'

Startled, she glanced over and met Damon's knowing gaze. He smiled at her and then looked down to his tablet, his fingers skipping over the keyboard.

She sat back, relaxing as she appreciated how hard he worked. People counted on him and he delivered. No wonder he'd become as successful as he had. An outlier—fiercely intelligent, gifted, and hard-working. But he liked to do things his way—in his place, in his time.

'It's looking good.' Damon rose and studied her page.

She chuckled and shook her head.

He pointed at the faint lines she'd drawn in. 'You've had training.'

'Well, drawing classes were quite an acceptable occupation for a young princess.'

'Until you wanted to get serious about it?' Damon was too astute.

Even she'd understood that it was impossible—as had her art professor. She still saw him sometimes. 'I used my interest to become knowledgeable about the art and antique treasures in the palace.' She stood and stretched, keen to get out to the warm sunshine. 'I like to take the tours sometimes.'

'As the guide?' Damon's eyes widened.

She nodded, laughing at his expression.

'No wonder they're always booked out so far in advance—they're all hoping to get on one of your days.'

'I don't commit to an exact timetable,' she admitted.

'Because you don't want to become an exhibit yourself.'

No. Trust him to understand that. And she hadn't wanted to disappoint people. She turned to get past him and head out to the beach.

'I don't see why it has to be only a hobby,' he said, still studying the incomplete drawing. 'You could sell them. People would buy them.'

Eleni laughed again. 'They'd sell only for the signature. There'd be no honest appraisal from anyone. Some fawning critics couldn't be objective for fear of offending the royal family while others would damn me to mediocrity for daring to think I could do something with skill.'

'You're afraid of what they think.' He sent her that stern look again. 'You don't need to give a damn, Eleni. You could sell them for charity. Imagine what you could raise.'

'But I do give a damn and so I raise money anyway. But I don't want this tied to that. This is my escape.' Just as this island was his.

'Then do it anonymously. We could find a dealer.'

'Or I could just do them for myself.' She sent him the stern look back. 'For my own enjoyment.'

'They'd bring joy to other people too,' he said charmingly.

'Flatterer.' She mock slapped him as she walked away.

'I have no need to flatter you when I already own your panties,' he called after her.

She stopped and swivelled to send him a *death* stare that time. 'Oh, that is—'

He threw back his head and laughed. 'True. It's true.'

* * *

Playing in the sea with Eleni was too much fun. She was so beautiful, lithe and, as he'd suspected that very first moment he'd seen her, strong. Now, as he sat on the sand beside her and let the sun dry his skin, satisfaction pooled within him. The same feeling that had crept up on him while she'd been seated beside him upstairs all morning.

But it was the quiet moments like these that unsettled him the most—when he felt too content.

Moments like these became too precious. And moments didn't last. Nor did marriages.

He stood, needing some space for a second to get them back to that light teasing. He turned and tugged her to her feet. He only had to whisper a dare and they raced back to the house. Play came so easy with her now she was free.

'How do you ever force yourself off this island?' she asked, breathless as he caught her.

'Actually we're leaving in the morning,' Damon muttered.

'What?' Her shocked query made him turn her in his arms so he could see her eyes.

'It's only twenty minutes by helicopter to the next island,' Damon quickly explained. 'There aren't many shops but...' He strode to a small cabinet in the lounge and retrieved a small purse that he tossed to her. 'Here. You can go wild, practise counting out the right currency before you hit the big cities.'

She caught the bag neatly with one hand but wrinkled her pretty nose. 'I don't want your money.'

'Well, until you earn your own I think you're stuck with mine, because I'm your husband and apparently that makes me responsible.' He sent her a deliberately patronising smile. 'I can give you an allowance if you'd like.'

The nose-wrinkle morphed into a full-face frown.

Chuckling, he backed her up against the wall. 'If our

positions were reversed, you'd do the same for me,' he whispered.

'Don't be so sure.'

'Oh, I'm sure.' Laughing, he kissed her.

But her lips parted and she didn't just let him in, she pulled him closer, hooking her leg around his waist, her towel dropping in the process.

'If you keep this up I'll get you a credit card, so you don't even have to count.' He rolled his hips against her heat, giving into the irresistible desire she roused in him.

'Payment for services rendered?' she asked tartly. 'Finally you've figured out I married you for your money.'

'I knew it.' He failed to claw back some semblance of sanity from the ultimate temptation she personified.

'It certainly wasn't for your charm.' She glared at him.

'Then spend every cent.' He smiled, loving the sparks in her eyes. Those few shops mainly stocked bikinis. The thought made his mouth dry. 'Meanwhile…' he stepped back and unfastened his shorts '… I was thinking you might want me to model for you.'

'You're…' Her gaze dropped and her words faded.

'You're not concerned about people taking photos?'

He shook his head as their helicopter descended. 'The people here appreciate the privacy of their visitors.'

To be frank, the island was barely larger than Damon's. There were only a few shops along the waterfront and, when Eleni saw this, her expressive features were a picture of mock outrage. He laughed, enjoying his little joke.

'They sell bikinis.' He held up his hands in surrender. 'I thought you'd love it.'

'You're the biggest tease ever.' She growled at him with a glint in her eye. 'You're the one who wants me to get the bikinis.'

'Have you ever bought a bikini before? All by yourself?'

'Actually I have. Online.'

'In the privacy of the palace.'

'Of course.'

'Well, you can cruise the whole mall here.'

She rolled her eyes.

'If you don't want to shop for skimpy little swimsuits, why don't you spend some coin and buy me an ice cream?' He dared her.

'Because you don't deserve it.'

She flounced off to the bikini store and he lazily loitered outside, watching her through the wide open doors as she browsed the racks. In less than five seconds she lost that faux indignance and relaxed. As she chatted to the woman serving behind the counter she relaxed even more and that gorgeous vitality oozed from her skin. His gaze narrowed as it finally clicked—*interaction* with others was what gave her that luminescence. The ability she had to be able to talk to anyone, and to put them at ease, wasn't just learned skill from being 'the Princess', it was a core part of *who* she was. Warm, compassionate. Interested. Caring.

So much more than him.

Now she'd stopped to talk to another couple of customers and she was positively glowing. One of the women was balancing a wriggling toddler in her arms. Damon watched as Eleni turned to talk to the child, who immediately stopped wriggling and smiled, entranced—as if Eleni was some damn baby whisperer. Of course she was—she had that effect on everyone, big and small. They stopped what they were doing and smiled when she came near. Because she was like a beautiful, sparkling light.

She was going to be such a great mother, given her truly genuine, generous nature. He narrowed his gaze as his imagination caught him unawares—slipping him a vision of how she was going to look when cradling their child in her arms. Primitive possessiveness clenched in his gut, sending a totally foreign kind of heat throughout his veins.

His woman. His baby. His world.

He blinked, breathing hard, bringing himself back to here, now, on the beach. Her body had yet to reveal its fertile secret—while her breasts were slightly fuller, her belly had barely a curve. But their baby was safe within her womb.

Despite the summer sun, a chill swept across his skin and he cocked his head to study her closer. The baby was safe, wasn't it? And Eleni. She was slim but strong, right? But icy uncertainty dripped down his spine—slow at first, then in a rush as he suddenly realised what he'd been too full of lust and selfish haste to remember.

Eleni's mother had lost her life in childbirth.

Damon felt as if some invisible giant had wrapped a fist around his chest and was squeezing it, making his blood pound and his lungs too tight to draw breath.

How could he have forgotten that? How could he have dragged her here to this remote island without seeing that damn doctor back in Palisades? He'd promised her brother that she'd get the best care, yet he'd been in too much of a hurry to escape his own demons to put her first. To put his child first.

He'd been thinking only of himself. His wants. His needs. His father had done that to Kassie and her mother. Now Damon was as guilty regarding Eleni and their unborn child.

How could he have neglected to tend to something so fundamental? He'd been so smug when he'd texted his assistant to find an obstetrician that day on the boat. As if he'd thought of everything—all in control and capable.

But he wasn't either of those things. Turned out he was less than useless—to not even have a routine check done before flying for hours out to somewhere this isolated? What the hell kind of father did he think he was going to make anyway?

He'd failed before he'd even begun. Both his wife and child deserved better. He huffed out a strained breath. At least seeing the truth now cemented the perfection of his plan. They'd be better off apart from him. He'd always known that, hadn't he? Wasn't that why he'd insisted on his and Eleni's separation in the first place?

This whole marriage and kids and happy-ever-after was never going to be for him.

Except, just for this little while on his island, he'd let himself pretend.

That he could have it all with her. Be it all for her.

But he couldn't.

Bitterness welled, a surging ball of disappointment within himself. For himself.

'Are you okay?' Eleni gave him a searching look as she joined him to stroll along the beach.

'Fine.' He flashed a smile through a gritted jaw and kept strolling along the beach, staring down at the sand.

But he wasn't and wasn't it typical that she'd already sensed that? She was too compassionate. Too empathetic.

'Did you spend up large?' He made himself make that small talk.

'Every cent.' She held up a carrier bag and shook it, a twinkle in her eye that he couldn't bear to see right now.

'Then let's go back,' he said briskly.

He sensed her quick frown but she simply turned and quietly walked alongside him.

Of course she did; that was Eleni all over—doing what was asked of her, knowing her place, unquestioning when she sensed tension.

It was how she handled Giorgos, how she handled the public and palace demands on her. And, apparently, it was now how she handled him.

It was the last damn thing that he wanted. He wanted impetuous, spontaneous, emotional Eleni who liked nothing more than to challenge him. But what he wanted no longer mattered. Because she was vulnerable and he didn't have the skills that she was going to need long term. He'd just proven that to himself. The lust they shared wasn't ever going to be enough and the sooner they separated, the better.

He was such a damn disappointment to himself—let alone to anyone else.

'I'm going to the workshop for a while,' he said the second their helicopter landed.

'Sure.'

He turned his back on that hint of coolness in her voice. The tiniest thread of uncertainty. Of hurt. He had to walk away to stop hurting her more. That was the point.

The guys were heads down, but he waved them away when he walked into the room. He'd rebalance in here. Get stuck in another of the projects. But while he could take in the info his team had sent him, he couldn't make it stick. The future kept calling—her pregnancy, the baby. What he was never going to be able to do for them both.

'Which do you want to go with?' Olly ventured over to Damon, showing him three designs for a new logo.

'I need to think about it.' Damon lifted the sheet displaying the three options, his gaze narrowing as he registered the colours. He wanted to do more than think about it. He wanted to ask Eleni. She had a better eye than any of them.

'I had a call from one of those futurist foundations,' Olly said as Damon headed to the door. 'They'd like you to speak at next year's gala.'

More like they wanted him to bring his beautiful Princess wife. He did *not* want her used that way.

'Next year?' Damon asked idly, still staring down at the sheet.

'They're planning well ahead of time. Futurists,' Olly joked.

Time. Damon walked out of the den. In time, according to Damon's plan, he and Eleni would be sharing custody but living separately. They'd be on their way to divorce already. She wouldn't be curled next to him in bed, or sitting at a desk at his side any more. And their child would be a few months old. Their tiny baby with its tiny heart would still be so vulnerable. His chest tightened. He had no idea how to provide the required protection. How did he protect Eleni? How did he give either of them what they needed when he hardly knew what that was? When he'd never had it himself?

Eleni had changed so much in the few days she'd had of freedom. He realised now how much more she needed. How much more she deserved. She was loving and generous and kind. She deserved someone who could give all that back to her tenfold.

She was going to be a far better mother to their child than his mother had been to him. She was open; she was generous. She was loving.

What did *he* have to offer her? She had a workaholic brother and no one else close in her life. She needed a husband who could offer her a warm, loving family. All he could offer were sycophantic grandparents who'd leech everything they could from the connection—and offer nothing. No warmth. No love.

Damon had money, sure. But King Giorgos would never let his little sister suffer financial hardship. There was nothing else he really had to offer her—other than orgasms and the occasional cheesy line that made her laugh. He didn't know how to be a good father, or a good husband. She deserved more than that. She deserved the best.

And he had to help her find that somehow. He owed her that much at least, didn't he?

He walked to the house, missing her already, wanting her advice on the decision he couldn't quite make, just wanting to be near her again. He found her at her desk—her new favourite place—clad in a vibrant orange bikini that was bold and cheerful and sexy as hell. She wore a sheer white shirt over it that hung loose and revealed a gently tanned shoulder. Her hair wasn't brushed into smooth perfection but looked tousled and soft and there wasn't a scrap of make-up on her glowing skin.

She looked beautiful and relaxed; he'd never seen her look happier. She was thriving, from so little. She should have so much more. More than he could ever give her.

Her welcoming smile pained him in a way he'd never been pained before.

'You're busy.' He hesitated, staying at a distance, trying to resist that fierce, fierce pull.

She deserves better.

'It's okay.' She put down her pen and turned her full focus on him. 'What did you want?'

He'd forgotten already. But her gaze grazed the paper he was holding.

'I just...' he glanced down at the images he held '...wanted your opinion on this.'

'My opinion?' she echoed softly.

'You have an artist's eye.' He gruffly pushed the words past the block in his throat. 'I wanted to know which you think is better.'

Eleni blinked, pulling her scattered wits together. He walked in here looking all stormy and broody and sexy as hell and then wanted her opinion on something he was clinging to as if it were worth his very soul?

'Are you going to let me see it?' She smiled but he didn't smile back.

He put the page on her desk. She studied the three designs that had been printed on it. That he valued her input touched her and it took her a moment to focus on what he'd asked her to do. 'I think this one is cleaner. It stays in the mind more.' She pointed to the one on the left. 'Don't you think?'

'Yes,' he said, nodding brusquely. 'Thank you.'

A defiant, determined look crossed his face as he stepped back from her. She stilled, trying to read all the contrary emotions flickering in his expression. He always tried to contain such depth of feeling, but right now it was pouring from him and she could only stare, aching to understand what on earth was churning in his head.

'What?' His lips twisted in a wry, self-mocking smile. 'I don't know why you're staring at me when you're the one with ink on her nose.'

'Oh.' Embarrassed, she rubbed the side of her nose with her finger.

He half snorted, half groaned. 'Come here,' he ordered gruffly, tugging a clean tissue from the box on his desk.

She loved being this close to him. Loved the way he teased her as he cared for her. She held ultra-still so he could wipe the smear from her face. He was so close, so tender and she ached for that usual teasing. But his eyes were even more intensely blue and his expression grave. He focused on her in a way that no one else ever had. He saw beyond the superficial layers through to her needs beneath. Not just her needs. Her gifts. He saw *value* in her and he appreciated it. That mattered to her more than she could have ever imagined. Suddenly, thoughtlessly, she swayed, her need to be closer to him driving her body.

'Eleni?' He gripped her arms to steady her, concern deepening the blue of his eyes even more. 'You okay?'

All the feelings bloomed in the face of the irresistible temptation he embodied—the capricious risk he dared from her with a mere look. But beneath it was the steadfast core of certainty. He'd caught her. Just as he'd caught her and held her close that very first night. Somehow she knew he'd always catch her. He was there for her in a way no one had ever been before. That spontaneous tide of emotion only he stirred now swept from her heart, carrying with it those secret words until they slipped right out of her in a shaky whisper of truth that she breathed between them.

'I love you.'

CHAPTER THIRTEEN

'I'M NOT SORRY I said that,' she said shakily, determined to believe her own words.

Impulsive. Impetuous. Spontaneous. *Stupid.*

Because he stood rigid as rock, his fingers digging hard into her upper arms and his eyes wide. But his obvious shock somehow made her bold. She could have no regrets. Not about this. Not now. So she said it again—louder this time.

'I've fallen in love with you, Damon.'

It felt good to admit it. Terrifying, but good.

His expression still didn't change. Just as it hadn't in the last ten seconds. But then he released her so quickly she had to take a step back to maintain her balance.

'You only think you're in love with me because I was your first.' He finally spoke—harsh and blunt. And then he turned his back on her.

That was so out of left-field that she gaped as he walked away towards his desk. 'Give me some credit.' She was so stunned she stormed after him and yanked on his arm to make him face her again. 'Even just a little.'

But he shrugged her hand off.

'Eleni, look...' He paused and drew breath. 'You've never felt lust before. You haven't had the opportunity until now. I'm just the first guy you've met who got your rocks off. But lust doesn't equal love. It never does.'

'Actually I do know that.' She wasn't stupid. And she didn't understand why he was lashing out at her. She was utterly shocked.

'Do you, Eleni?' He looked icier than ever. 'You've got freedom here that you've never had in all your life. I think you're confused.'

'Because I've been able to hang out at the beach without worrying about any photographers in the bushes? You think that's made me think I'm in love with you?' She couldn't believe he was saying this. 'I might not have had a million lovers, but I know how to care. I do know how to love.'

'No, you know how to acquiesce,' he said scathingly. 'How to do as you're told while suffering underneath that beautiful, serene exterior. While not standing up for yourself.'

'I'm standing up for myself now.'

He shook his head 'You're confused.'

'And you're treating me like the child my brother sees me as. You don't think I'm capable of thinking for myself?' Was he truly belittling her feelings for him? He didn't believe her and that hurt. 'This is real.'

'No, it isn't.'

'Don't deny my truth.'

'Eleni.' He closed his eyes for a second but then he seemed to strengthen, broadening his stance. He opened his eyes and his stark expression made her step back.

'I have used you. I have treated you terribly. You can't and don't love me.' He drew in a harsh breath. 'And I'm sorry, but I don't love you.' He seemed to brace his feet a bit further apart. 'We are only together now because you're pregnant.'

His words wounded where she was most vulnerable. Because underneath she'd known this had never been about *her*. He never would have sought her out again if he hadn't been worried about the contraception mistake that night. He'd never wanted to see her again—not just for her.

'This has only ever been for the baby,' she said softly.

'Yes. For its legitimacy and protection.'

'Yet you were happy to sleep with me again.'

His gaze shifted. Lowered.

He'd been happy to string her along. 'And Princess Eleni was an easy conquest because she was so inexperienced and frustrated it took nothing to turn her on…is that how this has been?' She couldn't bear to look at him now, yet she couldn't look away either.

'Eleni—'

'Maybe I was inexperienced and maybe I was starving for attention—' She broke off as a horrible thought occurred to her. 'Have you been laughing at me this whole time?'

Suddenly her skin burned crimson at the recollection of her unbridled behaviour with him. So many times.

'Never laughing.' His skin was also burnished. 'And I'm not now. But you *are* mistaking lust for deeper affection.'

She didn't believe him. She couldn't.

'So you don't feel anything for me but lust?' When he sat with her on the beach and they talked of everything and nothing? When they laughed about stupid little things?

There was a thin plea in her voice that she wanted to swallow back but it was too late. Maybe he'd been trying to keep his distance and now she'd forced him into letting her down completely. 'You don't think we could have it all?'

'No one has it all, Eleni. That's a promise that doesn't exist.'

'No. That's your excuse not to even try. It works out for plenty of people. Maybe not your parents—' She broke off. 'Is this what you learnt from them? Not to even try?'

'Yes.' He was like stone. 'I'm not capable of this, Eleni. Not marriage. Not for ever. Certainly not love.'

'You don't mean that.'

'Don't I?' He laughed bitterly. 'How can you possibly think you're in love with me?' He stalked towards her. 'I seduced you—an innocent. I knew you were shy that night. I knew you weren't that experienced. Did I let that stop me from taking you in a ten-minute display of dominant sex? No. It made it even hotter. But I got you pregnant. Then I kidnapped you. I forced you into marrying me. Tell me, how is that any kind of basis for a long-term relationship?' His short bark of laughter was mirthless. 'It will *never* work.'

'It wasn't like that.'

'It was exactly like that.'

No, it hadn't been. He was painting himself as a villain like in one of the games he'd once designed.

'You don't care about me at all?' She couldn't stop herself from asking it.

'Enough to know you deserve better.'

'Better than what—you?' She stared at him. 'You're more sensitive than you like to admit. More caring. You're kind to your employees, you've been kind to *me*.' She tried to smile but couldn't because this was too important and because she could already see he wasn't listening. And he certainly wasn't believing her. 'You're thoughtful, creative. And you think I don't mean it.'

'You only think you mean it.'

Could he get any more insulting? She'd prove him wrong. She glared at him. 'I know you don't want any part of royal life. You don't value what I am. So I will relinquish my title.'

'What?' He looked stunned—and appalled.

'I'll tell Giorgos that I want to live as a commoner. We could live anywhere then. Here, even. Maybe I could get a normal job, not just cut ribbons and talk to people. I could do something useful.'

He laughed.

Eleni chilled and then burned hot. He'd thrown it back at her—her love. Her proof. He was treating her as everyone else in her life had—as if she were a decorative but ultimately pointless ornament with no depth, no real meaning. No real value. When for a while there, he'd made her think he felt otherwise. That he saw her differently—that he thought she had more to offer. He'd shown her such caring and consideration. Hadn't he meant that at all?

'Why won't you believe me?' she asked him, so hurt she couldn't hide. 'Are you too scared to believe me?'

He just stayed frozen. 'You don't mean it, Eleni.'

'Why is it so impossible to believe that I could love you?' She demanded his answer. Because she was certain this rejection came from fear. 'Or that I could want to give up everything to be with you?'

'So now you think there has to be something wrong with me because I don't want your love?' he asked cruelly. 'Maybe you suddenly want to give up your title because *you* don't like being a princess.'

'Poor me, right?' she said bitterly. 'I have to live in a castle and wear designer clothes and have all these things—'

'You're not materialistic,' he interrupted harshly. '*Things* aren't what you want. What you *want* is out.'

'No. What I want is *you*.'

He stared at her.

'I want you with me,' she carried on recklessly. 'At the palace. Not at the palace. I don't care. I just want you there wherever I am. I want to know I have you by my side.' She totally lost it. 'I don't care what companies you own or what tech you help create. I just want the man who makes me smile. Who laughs at the same things I do. The man who's passionate and who, usually, can think like no one else I've met.' She drew in a short breath. 'What I'm trying to do is put you first. Put you ahead of my brother. My family. My duties and obligations. Don't you get it? I want *you*.'

'I don't want that,' he said harshly. 'I don't want you like that.' His eyes blazed. 'I'm not in love with you, Eleni. Don't you understand that I'll *never* be in love with you? And you'll soon realise you're not in love with me.'

She sucked in a shocked breath as his total rejection hit like a physical blow.

Hadn't the first rejection been humiliation enough? No. She'd had to go on and argue. But the fact was he didn't want to love her. He never had.

All their time together had been nothing but a physical bonus while he put up with their marriage to make the baby legitimate. Eleni was simply a temporary side issue.

She'd mistaken his affection and amusement for a growing genuine attachment, but the support he offered her was probably the kind he'd give any of his cool employees.

'I have to leave,' Eleni said dully. There was no way she could stay here with him now.

'You're going to run away?' he asked coldly. 'Because that's always worked so well for you in the past.'

No. She wasn't going to run away. In that one thing he was right. Running away never worked.

'This child is a *Nicolaides*.' She drew herself up tall. 'She or he will be royalty. And until Giorgos finally has a family of his own, she or he will be next in line to the throne after me. It seems there's no getting away from that. So I'm going to return to Palisades.' She was suddenly certain. And determined. 'That is where I belong.'

He stood very still. 'You won't see out these few months?'

If she hadn't believed that he didn't love her before, she did now. He had no emotion at all—no understanding of just how cruel that question was.

'I've just laid myself bare for you, Damon,' she choked. 'And you don't accept it. You don't accept me. You don't believe in me.' Her heart tore as she accepted *his* truth. 'You want me, but you don't love me. That's okay, you don't have to.' But bitterness choked her. 'One day, though, you are going to feel about someone the way I feel about you. And then you'll know. Because no one is immune, Damon. You're human and we're all *built* to feel.'

She stared hard at him as she realised what she'd failed to see before—and she hit him with it now. 'But what you feel most of is fear. That's why you hide away on your island paradise. Controlling every one of your interactions, having those brief affairs when you go to some city every so often. Keeping yourself safe because you're a coward. I get that your parents were less than average. I get that they hurt you. But don't use them as your excuse to back out of anything remotely complicated emotionally.'

She drew in a desperately needed breath. 'You don't think what I do has value—that I deserve more? Well, you're right, but not in the way you think. I help people. It may not be much, it may appear superficial, but in my role as Princess of Palisades I can make people smile. And I do deserve more. As a *person*. How can you possibly think I could stay here with you like this but not get all I need from you?' It would destroy her slowly and utterly.

The irony was *he* was the one to have shown her what she could have. What she'd hoped to have with him.

'You can't give me what I need, but I can't settle for less,' she said. 'So no, I won't "see out these few months". I can't stay a second longer than I have to.' Even though it was just about going to kill her to leave.

Eleni might never be loved personally. But as a princess she was. And that would have to do.

CHAPTER FOURTEEN

DAMON PACED ALONG the beach, waiting for her to finish packing. She couldn't leave soon enough. He'd spoken the truth. She didn't 'love' him. She was in 'lust'—with him a little, but mostly with the freedom he'd provided for her. It wasn't *him personally*. It was the situation. Any other man and she'd feel the same about him. It was only fate that had made Damon the one.

He clenched his fists, because she offered such temptation. She made him want to believe in that impossible dream. In her.

But it was better to end it now. The pain in her eyes had been so unbearable he'd almost had to turn away. He hadn't meant to hurt her. But she was inexperienced and naive and he realised now their divorce might hurt her more if they didn't part now. He didn't want to lead her confused emotions on.

She didn't look at him as she climbed into the helicopter that would take her back to his jet, and then to Palisades.

'I'll have rooms set aside for you,' she said regally. 'You may visit at the weekends, so we maintain the illusion of a happy marriage until after the baby is born.'

He *'may'*? His brewing anger prickled at her tone. 'And after?'

'You may visit whenever you want. I won't stop you from seeing the baby.'

Even now she was generous. His anger mounted more, but he contained it. She would care for their child better than he ever could. He understood that now. Because his father had been right—they were alike. Damaged. Incapable and frankly undeserving of love.

He couldn't damage Eleni or his child any more than he already had.

* * *

The sun and the sand mocked him. His team were abnormally quiet and left him alone. He stood it for only two days before summoning the jet. He needed to get further away. San Francisco. London. Berlin. Paris.

He wanted her. He missed her. But he did not love her. He did not know how to love. It was easy to stay busy in cities—to arrange endless, pointless meetings that filled his head with fluff. But people asked about the Princess and he had to smile and pretend.

She was better off without him.

His head hurt. His body hurt. His chest—where his heart should be if he had one—that hurt too. But he didn't have a heart, right?

Yet all he could think about was Eleni. He spent every moment wondering what she was doing. Whether she was okay. If she was smiling that beautiful smile at all.

She'd given, not taken. She'd offered him the one thing that was truly her own—her heart. He knew she'd never done that before. She'd been at her most vulnerable. And he'd rejected her.

But he'd had to, for her. Because he didn't deserve her love. He had no idea how to become the man who did. If she was freed from the marriage to him, she might find some other man to treat her the way she deserved. That would be the right thing to do.

Hot, vicious, selfish anger consumed him at the thought of someone else holding her. Of someone else touching her. Of someone else making her smile.

He didn't want that. He *never* wanted that.

He clenched his fist, emotions boiling into a frenzy. He had no freaking idea how to manage this. And that was when he realised—so painfully—how much he didn't want to let her go. He *never* wanted to let her go.

He logged into his computer, searching for somewhere to go and sort himself out for good. Far from Palisades.

Far from his own island that was now too tainted with the memories of her presence. He had to escape everything and pull himself together. But as he scrolled through varying destinations, his emails landed in his inbox.

There was one from the palace secretary.

Damon paused. It would probably be another schedule of engagements that they wanted him to approve or something. Unable to resist, he clicked to the email and opened it. But it wasn't a list. It was a concise couple of sentences informing him that Princess Eleni had seen the obstetric specialist of her choosing who'd written a brief report, the contents of which had been inserted into the email. In one paragraph it explained that the baby was growing at a normal rate. That the condition that had taken Eleni's mother was not hereditary. That the pregnancy posed no abnormal risk to her. That everything was progressing as it ought for both mother and baby.

His breath and blood froze. There was an image file attached to the email. Dazed, Damon opened it on auto. A mass of grey appeared. He looked at the arrow and markers pointing out a particular blob set in a darker patch in the middle of the picture. It was an ultrasound scan. It was his baby.

He tried to breathe but he just stared at that tiny, little treasure in the centre of his screen. It was there. It was real. It was happening. Heat swept through him in a burning drive to claim what was—

Mine.

Both hands clenched into fists.

Eleni.

The thought of her consumed him—her strength, her decisions, her role in all this. She was well. She was strong. She was safe. He ached to reach for her, ached to see her smile as she saw this picture—he just knew she'd smile at this picture. And the realisation rocked him.

Ours.

They had made this beautiful child *together*. That night she'd come with him and he'd claimed her and somehow in that insanely wonderful moment they'd created this miracle. It never should have happened—but it had. And Eleni was taking it on. She was doing her bit and she was doing it so damn well. And if he wanted to be part of that, *he* was the one who had to shape up. Seeing this now, reading Eleni's results, he realised just how much he wanted in and he burned with acidic shame. He'd missed so much already. He wished like hell he'd been there with her when she'd seen this doctor and when she'd had this scan. He should have been holding her hand for every damn second.

He bent his head, squeezing his eyes shut so he could no longer see the image on that screen. But the truth snuck in and stabbed him anyway. The fact was he had a heart. He really, truly had a heart and it hurt like hell. Because it was no longer his.

Eleni had it. It was all hers. He had to tell her. He had to apologise. He had to get her back. Groaning, he closed the picture file and read the doctor's report again. And again. Sucking in the reassurance that Eleni was healthy. Strong. Safe.

She'd asked if he was scared of love and at the time he'd refused to answer. He'd been utterly unable to. But now he faced the stark facts. He was terrified. Like a freaking deer in the headlights he'd simply frozen.

Frozen her out.

Where she'd been brave, proudly standing up to him, he'd been unable to admit, even to himself, how much he wanted her in his life. And when she'd unconditionally offered him everything she had, he couldn't believe her. No one had ever offered him that before.

Eleni had been right. He was a coward. He hid because it was easier. But in truth he was no better than his parents—putting all emotion aside for work. But she'd got under his skin and he'd been unable to resist—he'd taken everything she'd offered. He'd even convinced himself he was doing her a favour. He'd encouraged her to blossom and let all that sweet enthusiasm and hot passion out. He'd thought she'd needed freedom away from the palace. Freedom to take what she wanted—to ask for what she wanted.

And she had.

Eleni had offered him her love. And she'd asked for his in return.

But he'd rejected her. The worst thing he could have done was not take her seriously. Only he'd done even worse. He'd scoffed at her.

That hot streak of possessiveness surged through his veins as he clicked open that ultrasound image again. But he sucked in a steadying breath. He didn't get to be possessive, not without earning her forgiveness first. Not without begging to make everything better. And how did he get to her now she was back in that damn prison of a palace?

CHAPTER FIFTEEN

'ARE YOU SURE you're feeling up to this, ma'am?' Bettina asked Eleni carefully.

'That's what blusher is for, right?' Eleni answered wryly. 'And I still have quite the tan on my arms.' She forced a smile for her maid. 'I'm fine to go. It'll be fun. But thank you.'

She needed to fill in her day. She needed to feel *something*.

She'd been buried in the palace for almost a fortnight, hoping she'd hear from him. But she hadn't. She couldn't face drawing, couldn't face the pool. She'd tried reading. But her mind still wandered to him. She hated how much she ached for him.

He doesn't deserve me.

She tried to remind herself, but it didn't lessen the hurt. Hopefully this gallery visit would take her mind off him even for a few minutes. The fact that it was a children's tour was even better because children asked questions fearlessly—with no thought to privacy or palace protocol. It would be a good test. She'd have to hold herself together when they mentioned his name. And they would ask. They'd want to see her engagement and wedding rings. They'd want to see her smiling.

They expected a blushing, beyond happy bride.

Giorgos had sounded harried when he'd phoned, which was unlike him. And for whatever reason that he hadn't had time to explain, he was still residing at the Summer House and he'd asked if she'd attend the small gallery opening on his behalf. Of course she'd agreed. She'd been going insane staying inside. She needed to build a busy and fulfilling life. Then she could and would cope with the break in her heart.

But she'd appreciated the concern in Giorgos's voice. Just as she appreciated Bettina's quiet care. And her bodyguard's constant, silent presence.

She smiled as Tony opened the car door for her. 'It's nice to have you back.'

'Thank you, ma'am.'

'I promise not to disappear on you today,' she teased lightly, determined not to hide from the past.

'I understand, ma'am.' Tony's impassive expression cracked and he smiled at her. 'You won't be out of my sight for a second.'

'I understand and I do appreciate it.'

It was a beautiful late summer morning but she'd added a light jacket to complement the floaty-style floral dress she'd worn to hide her figure and deflect any conjecture and commentary. That suspicion would be raised soon enough. But preferably not today.

Twenty minutes later she stepped out of the car at the discreet side entrance of the new art space. She took a moment to accept a posy of flowers from a sweet young girl. But as she turned to enter the gallery she froze, her heart seizing. She blinked and moved as Tony guided her forward. But she glanced back as something caught her eye. For a second she'd thought she'd seen a masculine figure standing on the far side of the road—tall, broad, more handsome than Adonis...

Wishful, impossible thinking.

Because there was no man there now.

Releasing a measured breath, she walked with the small group of children through the new wing of the gallery, focusing her mind to discuss the paintings with them. But despite the easing of her morning sickness over the past few days, maintaining her spark during the visit drained her more than she'd thought it would. She was relieved when she saw Tony give her the usual signal before turning slightly to mutter into his mobile phone.

Damon had half expected soldiers to swoop on him and frogmarch him straight to the city dungeons, but the coast was clear and the path to the car easy. It was unlocked and he took the driver's seat, waiting for the signal. Anticipation surged as his phone rang. He could hardly remain still.

Finally the passenger door opened. He heard her polite thanks.

He started the engine. As soon as she'd got into the car and the door closed behind her, he pulled away from the kerb.

'Tony?' Eleni leaned forward in her seat.

'Damon,' he corrected, a vicious pleasure shooting through his body at just hearing her voice again.

He glanced up and looked in the rear-view mirror and almost lost control of the car in the process. She was so beautiful. But that soft colour slowly leeched from her skin as she met his gaze in the mirror and realised it truly was him. If he'd suffered before, he really felt it then. He'd killed her joy. The make-up stood out starkly against her whitened face. She'd had to paint on her customary vitality—her luminescence stolen. By him.

Her eyes were suddenly swimming in tears but she blinked them back. The effort she was expending to stay in control was immense. He hated seeing her this wretched. But at the same time, her distress gave him hope. His presence moved her. She hadn't forgotten him. Hadn't got over him.

He didn't deserve her.

'Why are you here?' She demanded his answer in the frostiest tones he'd ever heard from her.

All he wanted was to enfold her in his arms but he couldn't. She was furious with him and she had every right to be. He had to talk to her. Ask for forgiveness. Then ask for everything.

When he'd already rejected her.

He gripped the steering wheel more tightly as anxiety sharpened his muscles and he tried to remember where the hell he was going. Because this was going to be even harder than he'd imagined. And he'd imagined the worst.

'I'm kidnapping you.' He ground the words out, holding back all the others scrambling in his throat. He needed to get them somewhere that they could talk in private.

He glanced back at the rear-view mirror. Her emotion had morphed into cold, hard rage.

'I'm not doing this to Tony again,' she snapped, turning to look out of the window behind her to see if any cars were behind them. 'He'll be following. He doesn't deserve—'

'Tony knows you're with me,' he said quickly. 'So does Giorgos.'

She flicked her head back, her eyes flashing. 'So you planned this with everyone but me?'

He didn't want to answer more. He was only making it worse. Damn, it turned out he was good at that.

'This is *not* okay, Damon,' she said coldly.

'None of this is okay,' he growled, swerving around the nearest corner. 'And I can't wait—' He broke off and parked on one of the narrow cobbled streets.

'Can't wait for what?' she asked haughtily.

Eleni waited for his answer, trying to remain in control, but underneath her calm demeanour her heart was pounding and it was almost impossible to stop distress overtaking her sensibility. Damon was here. Not only that, he'd colluded with her brother and her bodyguard and she couldn't bear to think about *why*.

It mattered too much. *He* mattered too much.

But it was too late. He'd made his choice. He'd let her go. He'd let her *down*.

She refused to believe in the hope fluttering pathetically in her heart. This was too soon. She hadn't grown a strong enough scab over her wounds to meet him yet.

'Eleni.'

She closed her eyes. He couldn't *do* this to her.

One look. One word. That was all it took for her to want to fall into his arms again. She refused to be that weak. She couldn't let him have that power over her.

'Take me back to the palace,' she ordered.

He killed the engine. She watched, frozen, as he got out of the car and swiftly opened the rear passenger door. But before she could move he'd slid into the back seat with her and locked the doors again.

'Give me ten minutes,' he said, removing his aviator sunglasses and gazing intently at her. 'If you wish to return to the palace afterwards, then I'll take you there. I just want ten minutes. Can you give me that?'

She wanted to give him so much more already. But she couldn't. She'd been a fool for him already; she wasn't making that mistake again. 'What more is there to say, Damon? We want different things.'

'There's plenty more to say,' he argued shortly.

'Too late. You had your chance.' She glanced behind her, hoping Tony was less than a block away. But there was no car. No people.

'Ten minutes,' he pushed. 'I'm not letting you go until you listen to me.' He was silent for a moment. *'Please.'*

At that urgent whisper she turned back to face him. Starved of his company for days, she couldn't help drinking in his appearance now. He was studying her with that old intensity. Always he'd made her feel as if she were the only thing in the world that mattered.

Not fair. Not true. Not for him.

'Five minutes,' she answered flatly.

Only five. Because tendrils of hope were unfurling, reaching out, beginning to bind her back to him. That weak part of her wanted him to take her in his arms and kiss her. Then she might believe he was actually here. That he'd come back for her. But at the same time she knew that if he touched her, she'd be lost.

His smile was small and fleeting and disappeared the second he opened his mouth again. 'I'm so sorry, Eleni.'

Her heart stopped. Her breath died. She didn't know if she could take this. Not if he wasn't here to give her everything.

'Words said too easily,' she whispered.

'That night at the ball—'

'No,' she interrupted him furiously. 'We're not going back there. You're not doing this.'

'Yes, we are. It's where it all began, Eleni. We can't forget what's happened. We can't ignore—'

'You already have,' she argued. 'You already denied—'

'I lied,' he snapped back. 'Listen to me now. Please. That night was the most extreme case of lust I've ever felt,' he confessed angrily. 'And for you too. You know how powerful it was. How it *is*. You never would have let just any man touch you that way, Eleni. You never would have let just any man *inside*.'

She sucked in a shocked breath.

'I know I didn't want to admit it,' he said. 'But what's between us is something *much* more than that.' He gazed at her so intently, the blue of his eyes so brilliant it almost blinded her.

But she shook her head. Not for him, it wasn't.

'For me too,' he declared, rejecting her doubts. 'It was and is, Eleni. I've denied it for too long.' He bent closer, forcing her to look him right in those intense eyes. 'You were flirtatious, you were shy...so hot and so sweet.'

She winced. She couldn't bear for him to revisit her inexperience. Her naiveté. He'd thought she had nothing more than a teenage *crush* on him. He'd felt sorry for her.

'I belittled you when you told me your feelings,' he said.

'I didn't believe you. I couldn't…and I'm so sorry I did that to you.' Somehow he was sitting closer, his voice lower. His gently spoken words hit her roughly. 'I never should have let you go.'

'Why shouldn't you have?' She succumbed to the hurt of these last intolerably lonely days. 'You miss having my adoration? My body? My naive protestations of love?' She was so mortified. The imbalance was so severe. It was so unfair.

'Not naive.' He shook his head. 'Not you. *I'm* the ignorant one. I didn't know what love was, Eleni. I've never had someone give me what you've given me. And like the idiot I am, I didn't know how to handle it.' His gaze dropped. 'I don't know how to handle you or how I feel about you. It is so…' He trailed off and dragged in a breath. 'It's huge.' He pressed his fist to his chest. 'I was overwhelmed and I threw it away like it was a bomb you'd tossed at me.' His voice dropped to a whisper again. 'But the fact is, you'd already detonated my world. You took everything I thought I knew and turned it on its head. I thought I had it all together. The career. The occasional woman. The easy stroll through life. No complications. Every success was mine… but you made me *feel*.'

'Feel what?' she asked coldly, twisting her fingers together in her lap, stopping herself from edging anywhere nearer to him. She needed to hear him say so much more. She still couldn't let herself *trust*—

'Need,' he said rawly. 'Need to be with someone—to have you to talk to, to laugh with, to show everything, to hold, to just keep me company…to love…' He trailed off.

'So this is about *your* need?' She sent him a sharp look.

A harsh breath whistled out between his clenched teeth. 'I don't know how to be the kind of father that this baby deserves,' he gritted. 'I don't know how to be the kind of husband that you deserve. I have had awful examples of both and for a long time I believed…' Words failed him again.

Eleni didn't speak. She couldn't believe and it was becoming too hard to listen.

'I never imagined this would happen to me. And for it to be *you*?' He visibly paled. 'You deserve so much more than what I can give you.'

She shook her head, her rage surging. 'That's a cop-out, Damon.'

'You're a princess—'

'That's *irrelevant*,' she snapped.

'I don't mean your lineage. I mean in here.' He pressed his fist to his heart again but gazed at her. 'You're generous, loyal, loving, true…that's what I mean. You're not like other people—'

'I'm just like other people,' she argued fiercely. 'I'm human. *Most* people are loving and loyal, Damon. Most people are generous and honest.'

That was what he needed to learn and it crushed her that he hadn't learned it as he should have, that his life had been so devoid of normal family love.

'I'm nothing special,' she added.

'You're special to *me*!' he bellowed back at her. 'You're more generous, more loyal, more loving than anyone I've ever met and *all* I want is to be near you. You don't value yourself the way that you should.'

But she did now. She did, because of him. That was what he'd taught her. That was why she'd walked away from him. Because she knew what it was to truly love. And that she deserved more than he'd wanted to give her.

'Yes, I do,' she flung back at him brokenly. 'That's why I'm back in Palisades.' That was why she'd left him when it had almost killed her to do so. Because staying would have been an even more painful experience. She wasn't going to settle for less. Not now. Not from him. She couldn't exist settling for less from him. 'That's why I couldn't stay with you. Because I do need…'

The words stuck in her throat as the pain seeped out.

She knew he'd been hurt, but that he couldn't push past it for her? That hurt *her*.

He was staring into her eyes but his face blurred as her tears spilled—hot, fast, unstoppable, stupid tears.

'I'm so sorry, darling, so sorry I did this to you.' He reached out as she tried to turn away from him. His fingers were gentle as he captured her close and wiped the tears from her face. 'Please don't say I'm too late. It can't be too late. Because I love you, Eleni. Do you understand? I love you, I do.' He leaned closer as she remained silent. 'Eleni, please don't cry. Please listen to me.'

Her breath shuddered as she tried to still, needing to hear him.

His hands framed her face and he kept talking in those desperate hushed tones. 'Until you, I had no idea what love was—what it means, how to show it. And I want to love you, so much, but I don't know where to start. I don't know how to make this right. I'm begging you here, Eleni. How do I become the man you need?'

'You're *already* what I need,' she whispered hoarsely, so annoyed that he still didn't get it. 'You're everything I need. Just you. You're enough exactly as you are.' That was what he needed to learn too. 'And you have started.' She pushed past the ache in her throat. 'By showing up. By being here.'

By coming back for her.

He stared at her for a moment and then with the gentlest of fingertips he traced down her cheekbone. She struggled to quell her tremors at his tenderness.

'See? So generous,' he murmured, almost to himself. But then he cleared his throat and leaned that bit closer, his gaze fierce and unwavering. 'I love you, Eleni.'

Once again he said it. What she'd been too afraid to believe she'd really heard. And the words weren't whispered, they were strong, almost defiant.

He shook her gently. 'Did you hear me?'

* * *

Two more tears slowly rolled down her cheeks.

'I am so, so sorry it has taken me so long to figure it out. I miss you like—' He closed his eyes briefly but she'd already seen the stark pain. He opened them to stare hard at her. To try again. 'These past couple of weeks have been—'

That weak scab across her heart tore as he choked up in front of her. He couldn't find the words. She understood why—it was indescribable for her too.

'I know,' she whispered.

A small sigh escaped him. 'I don't deserve it, but please be patient with me. Talk to me. Talk like you did that hideous day you left me. I need your honesty… I just need you.'

She drew in a shaky breath, because she wanted to believe him so much. But she needed to understand. 'What changed? What brought you back?'

'Misery,' he said simply. 'I was so lonely and it hurt so much and I tried to escape it—you—but I couldn't. And finally I got thinking again.' He shook his head as if he were clearing the fog. 'I haven't been able to think clearly since that first second I saw you…it's just been blind instinct and gut reaction—equal parts lust and terror. I'd got *so* defensive and then, when I could finally think, I realised you were right. About everything. But I'd pushed you away. You're worth listening to, Eleni,' he whispered roughly, edging closer to her again. 'When you told me you loved me, I couldn't believe you… I was scared.'

'You don't think I was scared when I said it to you?'

The corner of his mouth lifted ruefully. 'You know my family doesn't do emotions. They do business connections. I want to do more than that, to be more…'

'You're more than that already. You just need to believe it.'

'I know that now. Because somehow, in all this, you *did* fall in love with me.' A hint of that old arrogance glinted in his eyes and his fingers tightened on her waist. 'You do love me.' His chin lifted as he all but dared her to deny it.

But she saw it in his eyes—the open vulnerability that he'd refused to let show before.

'Of course,' she said softly. 'I stood no chance.'

'Just as I stood no chance with you.' His hands swept, seeking as if he couldn't hold back from caressing her a second longer. 'And I'm afraid I can't let you go, Eleni. I can't live through you leaving me again.' He gripped her hips tightly. 'I'm taking you with me. I'm kidnapping you and I'm not going to say sorry for that.' Determination—desperation—streaked across his face.

At that raw emotion the last of her defences shattered.

'You're not kidnapping me.' She sobbed, leaning into his embrace. 'I choose to come with you.' Just as she'd chosen to be with him that first night. 'I choose to stay with you always.' She drew in a breath and framed his gorgeous face with her hands. 'I chose to marry you. I meant my marriage vows.'

'Thank God.' He hauled her into his lap with barely leashed passion. 'I love you. And I promise to honour you. Care for you…always.' He drew back to look solemnly into her eyes. 'It's not just a contract for me, Eleni.'

Her heart bursting, she flung her arms around his neck, kissing him with a hunger that almost overwhelmed her. 'I missed you so much,' she cried.

'Eleni.'

She heard the joy, the pure love in his voice. She felt it in his tender, fierce embrace and in the heat of his increasingly frantic kisses.

'I love you,' he muttered, kissing her desperately. 'I love you, I love you, I love you.'

It was as if he'd released the valve holding back his heart and now the most intense wave of emotion swamped her. Finally the veracity of *her* feelings could flow again. She had complete freedom to say what she wanted. To be who she was—who she'd wanted to be.

His lover. His beloved.

He held her so close, wiping away yet more tears that she didn't realise were tumbling down her cheeks. Opening her eyes, she saw a softness in his strong features that she'd not seen before. She trembled as she registered just how good this felt—how close she'd been to losing him. He'd been gone from her life too long. She needed his touch, his kiss, his hold—*now*.

'It's okay, sweetheart,' he soothed, kissing her again and again as she shuddered in his arms. 'It's okay.'

It was better than okay. It was heaven. And now she clung—unashamedly clung, needing to be so much nearer to him. 'Don't let me go.'

'Never again. I promise.'

But he'd hardly kissed her for long enough when he lifted his lips from hers and rested his forehead on hers, his breathing ragged. 'People are going to see us if we stay here too much longer…a palace car, illegally parked on the side of the road…'

'It doesn't matter.' Her voice rasped past the emotion aching in her throat. 'They know we're passionately in love.'

For real. Not just a fairy tale for the press. She ached to have him again completely.

He read her expression and groaned with a shake to his head. 'We can't be that reckless. And I'm crushing your pretty dress.' He lifted her from his lap, puffing out a strained breath. 'You're Princess Eleni, and this isn't right for you.'

She stilled, a thread of worry piercing her warmth. 'You don't like the palace.'

'I can learn to like it.' He brushed back her hair. 'I can learn a lot, Eleni. I can become the man you need. We can make it work.'

'You're already the man I need. You just need to stay—'

'Right by your side.' He met her gaze with utter surety in his. 'I know.'

Her eyes filled again. 'Where were you planning to drive me to?'

'Back to the boat.' A wry grin flitted across his lips. 'There aren't that many ways to kidnap a princess from Palisades. Damn palace is a fortress.'

She chuckled.

'But the treasure that was locked in there...' His old smug smile resurfaced. 'That's my treasure now.'

'And you're going to keep it?'

'Oh, I am. For always.'

'Then what are you waiting for? Let's get to the marina.'

His face lit up and then tightened in the merest split of a second. 'You can't imagine how much I need you—'

'Actually I think I can,' she argued breathlessly.

His laugh was ragged. 'You're hot and sweet, Eleni.' He swiftly climbed over to the driver's seat and started the engine.

'So, Giorgos and Tony were in on this?'

'I'm afraid so.' He drove quickly, confidently. 'You didn't stand a chance.'

'No?' she asked archly as he pulled into the park by the yacht.

'Believe it or not...' Damon got out of the car and opened her door '...they want you to be happy.'

'And they think being with you means happiness for me?'

'Does it?'

She stepped out of the car and reached up to stroke his face, seeing that hint of vulnerability flicker in his eyes once more. 'It does now, yes.'

He swiftly turned. 'We need to get on board. Now.'

'Are we going to sail off into the sunset?' She was so tempted to skip.

'Not for ever.' He winked at her. 'Palisades needs its Princess but I'll admit I'm going to push for part-time status.' He suddenly turned and swept her into his arms. With that gorgeous effortlessness he carried her across the boardwalk, onto the boat and straight into the bedroom. 'Because she'll be busy with her baby. And meeting the needs of her husband. And she'll be busy drawing and being creative with all the other things she's not let herself take the time for until now.' He paused, holding her just above the bed. 'Does that sound like a good plan to you?'

'It sounds like a brilliant plan.'

It was only moments until they were locked together. He was so close and she stared into his beautiful eyes.

'Take what you want from me, my beautiful,' he muttered. 'Anything and everything I have is yours.'

'I have your body,' she murmured. 'I want your heart.'

'It only beats because of you.' He laced his fingers through hers. 'I wasn't alive until I met you. You're everything to me. I love you, Eleni.'

'And I love you.' She wrapped around him, letting him carry them both into that bliss.

'Too quick,' he groaned, and gripped her hips tightly, slowing her.

Amused and beyond aroused, she tried to tease him. 'But what does it matter? We can go again, now we have all the time in the world.'

'Yes.' Those gorgeously intense eyes focused on her with that lethal desire and her heart soared as he answered. 'We have for ever.'

* * * * *

MILLS & BOON

Coming next month

KIDNAPPED FOR HIS ROYAL DUTY
Jane Porter

Before they came to Jolie, Dal would have described Poppy as pretty, in a fresh, wholesome, no-nonsense sort of way with her thick, shoulder-length brown hair and large, brown eyes and a serious little chin.

But as Poppy entered the dining room with its glossy white ceiling and dark purple walls, she looked anything but wholesome and no-nonsense.

She was wearing a silk gown the color of cherries, delicately embroidered with silver threads, and instead of her usual ponytail or chignon, her dark hair was down, and long, elegant chandelier earrings dangled from her ears. As she walked, the semi-sheer kaftan molded to her curves.

"It seems I've been keeping you waiting," she said, her voice pitched lower than usual and slightly breathless. "Izba insisted on all this," she added, gesturing up toward her face.

At first Dal thought she was referring to the ornate silver earrings that were catching and reflecting the light, but once she was seated across from him he realized her eyes had been rimmed with kohl and her lips had been outlined and filled in with a soft plum-pink gloss. "You're wearing makeup."

"Quite a lot of it, too." She grimaced. "I tried to explain to Izba that this wasn't me, but she's very determined once she makes her mind up about something and apparently, dinner with you requires me to look like a tart."

Dal checked his smile. "You don't look like a tart. Unless it's the kind of tart one wants to eat."

Color flooded Poppy's cheeks and she glanced away, suddenly shy, and he didn't know if it was her shyness or the shimmering dress that clung to her, but he didn't think any woman could be more beautiful, or desirable than Poppy right now. "You look lovely," he said quietly. "But I don't want you uncomfortable all through dinner. If you'd rather go remove the makeup I'm happy to wait."

She looked at him closely as if doubting his sincerity. "It's fun to dress up, but I'm worried Izba has the wrong idea about me."

"And what is that?"

"She seems to think you're going to…marry…me."

Continue reading
KIDNAPPED FOR HIS ROYAL DUTY
Jane Porter

Available next month
www.millsandboon.co.uk

LET'S TALK
Romance

For exclusive extracts, competitions
and special offers, find us online:

f facebook.com/millsandboon

⊙ @millsandboonuk

𝕏 @millsandboon

Or get in touch on 0844 844 1351*

For all the latest titles coming soon, visit
millsandboon.co.uk/nextmonth